Subway of Light

A Novel

by

Julian Bound

Because sometimes...
a second chance is all we need

ABOUT THE AUTHOR

Born in England, Julian Bound is a documentary photographer, film maker and author. With photographic work featured on the BBC news, his photographs have been published in National Geographic, New Scientist and in the international press. His work focuses on the social documentary of world culture, religion and traditions.

Living in Asia and South East Asia for over a decade, Julian travelled extensively throughout Tibet between the years of 2004 and 2014. Having lived in Dharamsala, India and Kathmandu, Nepal for four years, he studied meditation under the tuition of the Buddhist monks of Tibet and Northern Thailand and the spiritual teachers of India's Himalaya region.

With portraiture of His Holiness the 14th Dalai Lama, Julian has photographed the Tibetan refugee camps of Nepal and India. His other projects include the gypsies of Rajasthan, the Dharavi slums of Mumbai, and the sulphur miners at work in the active volcanoes of Eastern Java, Indonesia.

Present for the Nepal earthquakes of 2015 he documented the disaster whilst working as an emergency deployment photographer for various NGO and international embassies in conjunction with the United Nations.

Julian is also the author of the novels *'By Way of The Sea'*,
'The Geisha and The Monk' and *'Life's Heart Eternal'*.

CONTENTS

No one can tread your path but you, yet we should never dismiss those who join us from time to time on our journey.

CHAPTER ONE

A blur of red lights danced across a wet New York highway.

Through rain lashed windshield Sophia watched the cars ahead weaving from lane to lane in Friday evening rush hour traffic. She shook her head to their attempts of adding an extra ten minutes to a weekend of freedom. Her gaze leaving their race she looked to her husband and broke the silence between them.

"Well, Josh?"

"Well what?" He snapped, his eyes not leaving the hectic road.

"Shhh," Sophia hushed. "You'll wake the boys."

Turning to check if their father had woken them she smiled. They had not roused, embraced by their safety seats and wrapped up in matching fleece jackets as identical as the twins themselves. At the age of two years they had become oblivious to their parent's frequent arguments and continued to sleep on.

Sophia's dark brown eyes glared at Josh. With a brief glance back to the sleeping twins and then to him, she looked out into the autumnal night's heavy rain, her delicate features and shoulder length red hair highlighted in oncoming traffic's stark white headlights.

Sophia held her tongue, recalling how late at night from the nursery room door she and Josh would often watch the twins sleep.

'Best years of their lives,' they would joke, envious of their children's peace, not only with the world but also within themselves. The joking between them had ebbed away over the last few months. Now the idea of any kind of peace had turned into an obsessive wish, for them both.

"Dinner, tomorrow night," Sophia reminded her husband.

"No," Josh said. "I mean, I don't want to go," he added, aware of his abrupt tone.

"But I've made reservations." Sophia paused. She stared at Josh. "And managed to get a baby sitter."

She waited for a response, any response, yet none came. Looking to the window beside her, she tried to find some peace in the rain's silver creases trickling down its glass.

"Do you know how hard it is to get a sitter these days?" She pressed. "When was the last time we went out, just the two of us? Anywhere?"

A despondent Sophia looked back out into the night in Josh's silence, her bottom lip clenched tight between her teeth.

She couldn't understand where her husband had gone. Where was the wonderful man she knew, had met and fallen in love with? Sophia was strong. It had been her great inner strength that had attracted Josh to her from the first moment they had met. The irony now was that he put to test this quality he so admired within her.

Sophia was also patient, but she knew with all her strength of character that patience would not last forever and had begun to think what she had once believed unimaginable, taking the boys and leaving him.

Their car skidded slightly, jolting Sophia from her thoughts. She watched Josh sound the horn and mumble at the car they had just narrowly missed, projecting his own ineptness onto its driver to cover for his own mistakes.

The twins stirred. Their mother instinctively turned back to them.

"Be careful, Josh," she reached out to comfort the boys.

Both gave a soft murmur as Sophia checked the numerous buckles and straps holding them safe, relief arriving on watching tiny sleepy eyelids fall in a return to slumber.

"Remember how you used to say you'd always drive carefully?" Sophia returned to her seat. She began to smile. "Precious cargo you used to call us, remember?"

Her smile faded as Josh shrugged silently into the wet night.

It was then Sophia saw a glimpse of her husband's inner turmoil, his pain and remorse. These small glimpses were what had kept her faith in him and their future together over the past few months. They gave her the knowledge Josh was still there, somewhere. 'The real Josh was just hiding, he'll be back,' Sophia would reassure herself, and sometimes he was, albeit for the briefest of moments. These fleeting insights were what kept her by his side in hope the real Josh would return one day.

It broke her heart to see the husband she adored struggle and be so hard on himself. Sophia could not bear to see him so lost.

"I'm sorry, it's been a rough week," Josh said, his eyes still fixed on the road ahead.

Sophia reached over and placed a hand on his leg.

"Why don't you talk to your partners, Josh? See if you can take a break, just a little one. I'm quite sure they can design houses without you for a short while."

She gave his thigh a gentle squeeze.

"Just ask them, Josh, ask them to…"

Sophia stopped as her husband tensed beneath her fingers tips. Pulling her hand away, her body pushed back into her seat as the car accelerated.

They had argued about his beloved work as Sophia often called it more than anything else. The little time he already spent at home would mostly be taken alone at work in his study, coming to bed in the early hours of the morning, if at all.

Waking alone at dawn, Sophia would often find an exhausted Josh stretched across his desk, a computer keyboard serving as a makeshift pillow, a cold cup of coffee in an outstretched hand, its effects worn off long ago. Every time she would reach down with a tender kiss and usher him up to bed.

It pained Sophia to see the answers. To know a remedy for the hurt her husband contained, yet not be able to make him see what could release him from his anguish. Never before understanding when people said it was sometimes more lonely being with someone than actually being alone, that concept was becoming clearer to Sophia by the day.

"Why do you always have to bring my work up?" Josh snapped again.

Sophia tried not to retaliate, to keep her dignity. This time he had pushed her too far.

"Don't you ever talk to me like that," she counteracted with as much force.

Her fingers dug into her seat as the car accelerated once more.

"Where have you gone, Josh?"

"What the hell is that supposed to mean?"

3

"Well look at yourself. Why are you like this, so distant, so, so horrible?"

"I'm not. Not all the time."

Shame came to Josh. He knew he shouldn't be like this any time.

He wanted to tell Sophia how lost he felt, how much she and the boys meant to him. He just couldn't find the words within him. Nor could he find the reasons why something blocked him from telling her this. Josh was aware that through his actions he was slowly losing his best ally, his best friend and the love of his life. Searching within he still couldn't understand the barriers stopping him from telling his wife how much he cared, how important she and the boys were to him.

It felt he had lost something, that a part of him he used to treasure was gone. It had come to the point where he no longer recognised what that part was anymore, but he knew he missed it dearly.

"It's all here, we're all here," Sophia continued. "Josh you have all you need."

Ignoring his wife's pleas, he continued his vacant stare into the night ahead.

"Josh slow down."

He didn't hear his wife's frantic calls, or notice the twins stir in the back seat once more. Steeped in his own torment he tried to release the numb, lost feelings hounding him now.

"Slow down," Sophia shouted, at last breaking Josh from his trance.

It was too late. Both stared at the rear lights of the car in front burning bright in alarm and rushing towards them.

Touching the brakes Josh underestimated the slipperiness of the road now wet after a long hot summer of scorching heat, its surface now holding an ice rink sheen.

The back of their car slid out from behind them. Counteracting with an instinctive pull on the steering wheel in the opposite direction his reactions proved too slow. Wheels locked in place, they continued to career forward through the night's heavy rain. Josh winced to the sickening thud of metal upon metal as they struck the stationary car in front.

Sophia, Josh and the boy's defied gravity as the rear end of their car raised high above them. Flipping over the car levelled out, hurtling them upside down through the air above the ground.

Bewilderment played across the twin's wide eyes. They looked to their parents, searching for some sign of normality, willing them to make this all go away. Sophia turned to them. She stopped, becoming caught in Josh's gaze.

They stared intensely to each other the way they had always done. Two people sharing a life together, wrapped up within one another's love, the way they felt it had been every lifetime when they had found each other again.

Reaching out to touch Sophia, Josh broke their timeless spell and the present moment caught up with them in an instant.

As the inevitable road raced up towards them, Josh wanted to be held safe in Sophia's eyes once more, to tell her what he found so hard to say.

He knew there was no time for those words as he felt the impact of car and road, heard a crunch of steel and musical twinkle of broken glass around him, and then, darkness came.

CHAPTER TWO

The subway car was like any other. Universal train smells of dust and metal hung in the air over worn plastic seats and a slight breeze whipped through its open doors. The pages of a discarded newspaper fluttered on one of the seats and an empty coffee cup blew across the floor. In an extended arc it rolled down to the end of the carriage and came to a rest at Josh's feet. Looking down to the cup he raised his head.

Josh had no idea how he had arrived here, or how long he had been sitting alone in the scratched orange seat at the back of the subway car. It could have been three minutes or three days for all he knew.

Calm and as if nothing could bother him, Josh stretched out. Feeling the snug fit of his Upper Manhattan tailored suit and listening to the creak of Italian leather shoes below him, he leant back with both hands behind his head.

Looking around the empty subway car he noticed a subtle glow came from its metal lined walls and ceiling. He stared up at neon lighting strips for a clue to the train's radiance. The lights hummed above him and gave no answers. Josh looked to the window beside him trying to see at which station he now sat. Knowing the station was operational by its bright lights, there were neither signs, maps nor people on its platform.

Although Josh considered this unusual he remained seated, encircled by a sense of wellbeing. It felt right for him to be sitting here, like this was where he was supposed to be. Leaning forwards his elbows rested on his knees and bowing his head he smiled to the floor.

Another draft of air ruffled the newspaper a few rows from him. Its pages lifted then settled back down and Josh rose to his feet to retrieve its sheets. Maybe they could offer some clues as to where he was, or somehow tell him how he had arrived here in the first place.

He sat back down before taking a single step, startled by a small childlike giggle echoing throughout the subway car. Josh looked in the direction of the laughter, and then to its owner.

A small boy in striped T-shirt and jeans knelt up on his seat at the far opposite end of the carriage. The child's mop of brown hair shook as he giggled once more. Raising a small hand he waved across to Josh. Forgetting about the newspaper Josh waved back, not understanding why he had not noticed this young passenger before. Had he been there all along?

The boy remained in his seat and continued to smile over at him.

Guessing him to be around nine years old, Josh waved to him again before turning his attention back to the empty platform. Gleaming white tiled walls greeted him through the subway car's window as he tried to decipher where he was.

Wisps of cool air played across his cheek and he remembered the newspaper. With thoughts returning back to its pages Josh became distracted by the shuffle of feet at the far end of the carriage. Without a word, three figures walked down the aisle before coming to a stop at the subway car's exit in the middle of the carriage. Each faced the platform.

A middle-aged woman held the hand of the young girl next to her, both overshadowed by the imposing older man stood behind them.

They seemed unaware of Josh's presence until the young girl looked over and smiled at him. Josh stared back, puzzled by the appearance of these new passengers.

Tugging on the woman's hand the young girl pointed Josh out to her. Following the child's directions the woman looked over to him.

As the young boy giggled from the back of the subway car the young girl laughed with him. The woman looked back out onto the station's platform.

Her calmness faltered and she turned to the man behind her. He bent down and whispered something in her ear. Her peace regained he gestured to the subway car's open doors as the station began to fill with a pure white light.

The young girl released her hold and stepped out onto the

platform, encouraging the woman to join her. Moving forward to follow the woman stopped and glanced back at the man.

"Thank you," she said to him.

Turning her head to Josh, her eyes gave him a moment of reassurance before she faced the station and the eager young girl awaiting her arrival onto its platform.

the woman's eyes sparkled and she too began to laugh as if seeing something joyful beyond the subway car doors. With no hesitation she joined the young girl on the platform.

Remaining on the train the man waved to them both as the woman and the girl became shrouded in light. He stepped back as the subway car hissed and its doors closed in front of him.

The train began to move. Watching the glowing station flow from him Josh stared out into the darkness of the tunnel now entered. His fellow passenger continued to face the doors.

A shudder ran through the subway car as it began to accelerate, prompting the man to turn to Josh and slowly walk towards him.

With each deliberate step he placed a hand on the back of the seats to steady himself as the train swayed along its tracks until he at last stood before Josh.

With some apprehension Josh straightened and looked up to the one who had approached him.

"Hello, Josh," the man smiled down to him. "I've been waiting for you."

CHAPTER THREE

The man gestured to the seat beside Josh.

"May I?" He asked.

Glancing to the empty seat, Josh nodded and studied the stranger who lowered himself down beside him.

Though his lineless features bore no existence of years, Josh guessed him to be in his early sixties, yet it was his eyes that caught his attention, the kindest he had ever seen, a piercing blue that glistened like pools of Pacific waters.

"Do I know you?" Josh said.

The man offered his hand.

"My name is, George," he said, his words more statement than reply.

Josh reached over to receive his welcome. The lights flickered throughout the subway car as the two strangers touched and a small tingle ran up Josh's arm. He withdraw his hand in surprise.

"How do you know my name?" Josh rubbed his fingers as the sensation lingered on.

George looked across the subway car before turning back to Josh.

"How do you feel, Josh?" He asked.

Josh looked at the man that seemed to know him so well.

"Fine," he said after a brief pause.

"No, Josh. How do you really feel?"

Ready with a quick retort for the stranger something stopped Josh's words. George's question had delved deep within him, touching places he would often always keep closed to everyone, even himself. To his surprise Josh began to open up and disclose to his fellow passenger how he really felt.

"I feel like, like I'm supposed to be here." Josh looked around the train. "I don't know why, but I do. As if all this is right, the way it should be."

"Good, this is the best way to be." George leant back in his seat.

"I'm sorry, but do I know you?" Josh said. "You clearly know me from somewhere, but I'm afraid I can't remember you at all."

George took a moment before speaking.

"And what can you remember?"

"Huh?"

"I want to know what it is you can remember."

Josh looked to George. He seemed harmless enough, just some lonely old guy riding the subway with nothing better to do.

"Ok, ok," Josh decided to play along with his little game. "I remember meeting you, the station filling with light, whatever that was, a power surge or something. I remember the lady and her kid, and that other kid who waved at me."

"And, Josh?"

"And what?"

"What else do you remember?"

Growing tired of the old man's questions Josh shook his head.

"I can remember sitting here in this seat, alone, there was the newspaper, and…" Josh stared at George. "That's it, that's all I can remember. I know my name is Josh, I'm thirty three, but that's it."

Sitting up he tried to remember something before he had found himself on the subway car. Nothing came to him.

"What's happened to me? Why have I lost my memory, have I been in some kind of accident or something?" Looking to George for answers his eyes brightened. "Wait."

Reaching into his jacket he then rifled through his other pockets.

"It's gone."

"What has gone, Josh?"

"My wallet. Surely I must have a wallet with some ID telling me who I am, cards, money."

Josh checked through his pockets once more.

"You will not be needing money where we are going," George told him.

Josh froze, his hand still in his jacket pocket.

"What? Why, where are we going?"

His eyes shot around the subway car. His view stopped at its doors.

"No, I'm done here," he said. "Look, it was very nice meeting you, but I've got to go."

"Go where?"

"Off this train, where do you think I mean?"

"Josh, you could have left this train at any time before. The doors where open to you all along, but you choose to stay. Why was that?"

"I don't know, it felt right to stay I guess."

Worry entered Josh and he began to stand.

"Anyway, that was then," he said.

"No, not yet," George whispered.

As bewildered thoughts and emotions spun round Josh and his breathing became laboured. Sitting back in his seat he leant forwards.

George watched nausea settle within Josh. Reaching out to him he placed a hand onto his shoulder. A great calmness began to flow through Josh. His breathing regular once more he looked to George with a renewed feeling of peace.

George smiled as Josh eased beneath his touch.

"Who are you?" Josh stared back at him. "What are you?"

"Consider me as a guide."

"A guide? A guide to what?"

"A guide to yourself," George removed his hand. "Your memory will come back, do not worry. Slowly at first, but it will return. It just takes a little time. You all take time."

"All take time? There are others?"

"Oh yes, there are others. You have to remember one thing."

"And what's that?"

George paused for a moment.

"That it is not all about you," he replied.

Hypnotized by George's unexpected words, Josh began to consider that maybe what he was being told could actually be true. George held his new companion's bemused stare and began to speak.

"Josh, sometimes we can become so wrapped up in what we want, so enamoured by our own personal goals and ambitions that we forget who and what is around us, what is real, be it strangers, acquaintances or more importantly, loved ones."

Josh stirred in his seat. He glanced to the subway car doors and then back to George as he continued.

"Before we can consider another's ideas, we must first be aware that we have to listen, to take on other's points of view. For to not listen is where we first begin to stumble."

"Stumble?"

"Stumble into believing that we are the ones who are always right. That it is our way…"

"Or the highway."

"Yes Josh, exactly."

Josh began to question George.

"But what about drive? Ambition? Doesn't that count for anything?"

"Do not get me wrong, drive and want is inherently a good quality to have. It stops us from becoming stagnant, mundane even," George nodded. "Yet, to forget all in our sole pursuit for personal triumphs and gains leaves us with little but hollow victories." George looked out onto the empty subway car. "For sometimes when we attain our goal, reached that place where we have single mindedly strived to be, we are often left to wonder with whom there is to enjoy these spoils. Because Josh, the individuals who were around us as we strove to capture our dreams have often been forgotten, passed aside as we endeavoured to reach our own aspirations of where we wanted to be."

George's kind blue eyes found Josh once more, and although his memory had still not returned, George's selfless words had struck a nerve within him. Josh remained silent. He looked around the subway car and then to the floor. After a few moments of thought, he lifted his head to George and began to grin.

"Look, who's put you up to this? Whoever it was, nice trick." Josh said out to the subway car. "Where's the hidden camera?"

"Camera?"

"Yeah, camera, where is it?"

Josh's eyes scanned the carriage's walls and ceiling.

"I am sorry," George shook his head. "There is no camera. There are no tricks being played here."

Fear began to nestle in the pit of Josh's stomach and he looked to the window beside him.

Staring out into the tunnel's black void he once again tried to remember something, anything about himself. A terrifying thought entered him.

Lost and confused he looked to the subway car. Across its rows of seats he tried to find somewhere for his mind to escape to. Only the carriage's glow filled his sight and he turned back to George.

"Am I..." He stopped. Afraid to ask the question he so much needed to know the answer to.

"Are you what, Josh?"

"Am I... Have I died?" He finally found the courage to ask.

"That, I'm afraid I do not know the answer to."

"You don't know? What do you mean you don't know? What's going on here?"

George watched Josh's eyes well with tears.

"Let me explain," he said.

The train jolted and then returned to its usual rhythmic pattern. Easing back in his seat Josh waited for George's explanation.

"Josh, you have been taken out of your life."

"Taken?"

"Yes taken, to join me here on this train." George swept his hand across the carriage. "You see, this is what I do, I meet people like yourself. This subway car and the tracks we travel upon have been chosen for you. Somewhere you are, or were once familiar with. A metaphor so to say for you take this journey."

Josh sat attentive as George continued.

"Each person has their own special unique setting in which they are comfortable. Be it a car, the countryside or even an office block, everyone is different, yet you all share the same common factor. You are all on a journey, with me as guide, companion and hopefully, friend."

Josh looked to the rear of the subway car and tried to comprehend the stranger's words.

"If all this is true, then where are we going exactly?"

George settled back in his seat and began to explain more of their intended journey together.

"This subway train, your subway train, Josh, will take us along several stops. Some may seem familiar to you, some maybe not, but each will be as individual and significant as the other."

"And the destination?"

"That I am afraid I do not know the answer to. It may well be up to you."

The train began to slow.

"Up to me?"

"Acceptance is the key here. Learn to just be, to live in the present moment of the here and now. This state of mind will make your trip not only easier, but also more enjoyable."

George saw Josh had yet to fully grasp this concept.

"Josh, imagine a child at play. He or she neither thinks of the past or the future, they just concentrate on the present. What is before them at that moment in time. With no thoughts of what may happen or has happened, they remain in the here and now just being."

Josh looked to the far end of the subway car.

"The young boy," he remembered. "Where is he?"

Josh could not understand where he had gone. He had not seen him leave the subway car.

"Maybe we will see him again too," George said.

The train continued to slow, its melodic buzz lowering in pitch as George rose to his feet.

"Come on we are here, your first stop." George sensed Josh's anxiety. "You only need to take a leap of faith," he smiled.

Something in George's words soothed Josh's unease and he followed George along the subway car's aisle until they stood together at its exit.

As the train came to a halt he looked out through dusty windows then nervously to George.

"Just be," George winked as the doors swished open before them.

CHAPTER FOUR

George stepped out into the cool breeze drifting through the deserted station. As small whirlwinds of dust chased their tails beneath empty platform seats Josh joined his side on grey tiled flooring. He glanced back to the subway car's clicking and whirring as it cooled down on the tracks of its temporary new home.

"Ah, there it is," George lifted his chin to the exit sign along the platform. Striding towards the opening below it his enthusiasm spilled over into Josh, who still not entirely sure what was going on, began to share George's eagerness to see what lay ahead.

"After you," George said.

Josh stared down the entrance of the dark passage way. A dimly lit doorway beckoned them at its end. A sense of adventure overcame him and with a fleeting look to George he entered the corridor.

Walking together in silence their footsteps echoed across curved tiled walls. The light at the end of the passageway grew stronger on their approach and the temperature rose around them.

Josh stopped as a blurred shape crossed the doorway in front of them. Edging closer others began to pass by. Those hazy outlines formed into figures.

"There are people," he said.

"Yes, there are, but they cannot see us. You see we are not really here. We are merely observers. Although sometimes our physical presence can be felt."

"No one can see us? No one at all?"

"Well, there are those who are more sensitive and susceptible to the world around them, yet they are far and few between. Acceptance, remember, Josh?"

A cow's cumbersome body ambled past the doorway, blocking both light and heat from the busy street scene beyond.

"We must always be ready to expect the unexpected," George said as light beamed back into the tunnel. "Come on, just a few more footsteps."

With a deep breath Josh stepped out into bright midday sunlight.

Lined with restaurants and small shops a single street stretched out on either side of them.

"Watch out," George called.

Josh spun round and came face to face with another cow.

With red powder daubed on its forehead between horns adorned with garlands of flowers the cow closed in on them.

"Can it see us?"

"Oh yes, she can see us all right, but it is we who are going to have to move,"

Taking Josh's arm they both jumped into the dusty street.

"But I thought you said we couldn't be seen?" Josh watched the cow walk nonchalantly from them, oblivious to everyone and everything around her.

"Yes I did, but she is a cow."

"Huh?"

"Cows, cats, dogs or any other animal come to that, all have the ability to see us here. For they all live in the moment Josh. To them there was no yesterday, nor will there be a tomorrow. They just are. There is only the present, the here and now." George and Josh watched other pedestrians move from the cow's path. "Let us continue, there is so much to see."

George began to walk up the busy street. With a quick glance back to their arrival point Josh left the passageway behind him.

Breathing in the smells of sweet spices penetrating the air, they passed by hungry locals gathered around ramshackle mobile kitchens. Josh watched as they pushed and laughed amongst each other, eager to try the soups, dhal and rice on offer.

Continuing past restaurants playing loud music to attract its customers, Josh paused and looked to an old woman sat in front of one of them. Her dark creased face revealed a myriad of lines as she smiled up to passersby, encouraging all to buy trinkets and small brass statues from the dusty blanket laid out before her.

Josh looked to the old man beside her. Perched on a small stool and surrounded by an assortment of shoes, he bent over a worn anvil focusing intently on the large boot upon it. Reaching over to a pile of small strips of car tire he carefully choose a piece before attaching it to the sole of the boot, giving it a new lease of life with the aid of glue and small tacks hammered in by arms of taught sinewy muscle.

Leaving his view of the man, Josh saw George had continued onwards and now waved to him from the top of the street. Insecurity towards his new surroundings stirred in Josh and he hurried to him past more foreign smells and sights.

"Well, what do you think?" George greeted him.

Relieved to be beside George once more, he found that although his circumstances proved to be so bizarre he was beginning to enjoy the experience and felt caught up in his adventure.

"Where are we?" He asked.

"We are nearly there, Josh," George said with another wink and walked on.

Becoming used to George's ambiguity it did not bother Josh. He felt safe, secure as if nothing could harm him with this man by his side. Together they rounded the corner onto a peaceful stretch of road where a small market replaced busy restaurants and souvenir shops.

They walked by racks of exotic vegetables and tables piled high with fresh meat, each with homemade bread overflowing from dirty wicker baskets beneath them. Josh looked to a young woman dressed in a bright coloured sari. Sat on the floor behind a white sheet covered in an array of fish, flies fought for place amongst her wares only for an intricate henna detailed hand to brush them away with a fine tree branch, its hypnotic sway flowing from left to right above rows of glazed eyes.

As the market petered out and began to give way to more restaurants Josh noticed only a handful of customers sat at their tables.

"Look," George nodded across the street. Previously obscured by guesthouses and bars a large lake came into view.

The lake's flat, tranquil waters stretched out for miles to form the shape of a large teardrop. A small island lay off its banks surrounded in mist. As Josh peered closer he saw that mist was incense burning vigorously from a shrine within the island's centre. Brightly coloured rowing boats of blue, red and green emerged out of the smoke, each one ferrying devotees and tourists back and to from the mainland.

Fascinated by such a sight, Josh watched as they disembarked next to a group of women knee deep in water surrounded by tall bulrushes. The women laughed and chatted over piles of laundry, which they beat and pounded across large rocks worn smooth from centuries of use, pausing only from their work to hoist the triangular sheet slung high across their backs, each with a small child contained within.

A forested hill rose above the lake. Josh shielded his eyes and focused on the temple at its summit. There above the trees, the temple's white walls enhanced its golden rooftop sparkling in the sun's harsh glare.

"Let us stop a while," George said. "This place looks as good as any," he pointed to the restaurant beside them.

With a quick glance back to the temple, Josh followed George up three stone steps and onto a raised outdoor platform.

"Here will do," George sat at one of the tables and chairs laid out in neat rows giving them an ideal view of both restaurant and lake. Taking a place next to George, Josh looked back to the temple.

"That is not the reason we are here," George told him. "Look around you."

Keen to know the reason for their presence, Josh's view left the hillside and he looked around the small restaurant.

Between the hanging pots and pans of a small open kitchen, a young waiter flirted innocently with a bashful waitress. Josh could see her secret joy from his affections, unlike her father, the restaurant's owner. His stern looks put paid to the amorous young waiter, only to increase the blushes of his daughter. Smiling to the scene playing out before him Josh turned to the restaurant's few customers.

Sat at one table an elderly couple enjoyed the view of the lake in comfortable silence, their hands held tight within the others. At the table beside them a much younger couple showed all the signs of having just met as they shared stories, laughed, and smiled, breaking the ice as they discovered one another.

George nodded to the table at the opposite end of the restaurant. Josh looked over to its sole occupant.

A young man in his late teens sat writing in a dog-eared journal as travel worn as his T-shirt, jeans and flip-flops. Josh and George watched on as he looked up on occasion from beneath a mop of brown hair to sip from either the mug of steaming hot coffee or large bottle of water before him. Josh felt drawn to the young man, yet he couldn't understand why as the laughter of the newly acquainted couple and re-emergence of flirting staff all faded far into the background.

The young man wrote on unaware of the world around him until something broke his concentration.

"Here we go," George whispered to Josh, encouraging him to keep watching.

The young man before them raised his head. He reached for his coffee and then stopped. Seeing what had caught his eye Josh smiled, as together he and the young man watched a young woman walk down the street towards them.

Looking out onto the lake as she walked, the young woman turned her head to see in which direction she was going. She noticed the young man ahead. Her pace slowed briefly as she glanced to the floor and then with head held high continued to walk forwards.

The same age as he, her long red hair flowed behind a confident stride as she approached the restaurant. Stopping at the tall menu stand beside the young man's table she leafed through pages of Asian and western dishes. She glanced up at him. The young man gave her a faint smile. The corners of her lips rose coyly in return.

With crimson cheeks the young woman buried herself back between the pages of the menu and continued to browse through its contents. Flipping through its laminated sheets she peeked up at her spectator, he too began to blush. Closing the menu, the young woman looked back up to the young man and smiled to him once before walking away with a toss of red hair.

Watching her leave the young man shrugged with disappointment, and reaching for his coffee glanced back to where he had last seen the young woman. Catching a glimpse of her as she turned the corner of the street he returned to his writing, intent on getting whatever thoughts flowed through him out into the world.

From the other side of the restaurant Josh was enthralled by the young couple's short encounter.

"Was that it?" he said, holding a similar disappointment as did the young man.

"No, Josh. The show has only just begun. You will see, just keep watching."

Sensing something special was in the air Josh was eager to see what was about to be unveiled before him.

George sensed Josh's curiosity rise.

"We are seldom aware," he said. "What fragile moments new beginnings can be."

CHAPTER FIVE

Soft white clouds rolled across blue skies to cast a welcomed shadow over the town. Refreshed by the lakes accompanying cool winds, Josh watched its surface ripple then looked to the entrance of the restaurant.

The young man had left his writing and now watched the young red haired woman bounce up the stone steps and sit at the table opposite him. He smiled to her once more, trying to hide the surprise and delight of her return. Looking to him she gave another coy smile.

"Namaste," she said.

"Namaste," he replied.

"Brooklyn?" The young woman frowned and pointed to him.

"Yeah, you too?"

She nodded with a slight blush.

Josh held his breath at the pause between the strangers. He exhaled as the young woman spoke once again.

"I'm so thirsty," she said.

"Well, if you've got a glass," the young man reached over to the large water bottle beside him.

"Hell no," she said. "I need a beer."

Staring at her the young man laughed. Aware of her frankness the young woman joined his joy and tried to catch the waiter's attention. The staff continued to gaze dreamily at each other at the other end of the restaurant and taking matters into her own hands the young woman walked over to them.

As she passed by him and George, Josh looked back to the young man watching her approach the bar delighted by his new encounter.

Josh saw something had clicked between these two young people during their brief moment of laughter, as if something had fallen back into place.

"Can I join you?" She soon returned beer in hand.

"Yeah sure," the young man cleared the table to make room for her.

Wary at first, they became more comfortable with each other as their afternoon filled with laughter wore on. Josh picked up pieces of their conversation, but paid little attention to the words. The warmth these newly acquainted strangers emitted was far more enjoyable.

"Some people come together," George said.

Understanding his words, Josh knew this was not just a meeting of two people who exchanged pleasantries or passed the time together. He was aware that here before him something quite special was at play.

Over plates of food and reams of drinks the two talked and listened intently to each other's tales of where they had been, what they had done, and their dreams of the future.

The young man told of his studies in architecture and how he had taken time out to travel before returning to his second year at university. She in turn had left her courses in graphic design to travel and was toying with the idea of nursing as a new career.

Listening to the dreams and aspirations of the young, Josh tried his best to recall how he had felt at their age, wondering if he too had exuded the feelings of hope for the future these two held. Once again he drew a blank. He was just here, wherever here was, and could still not remember a thing past being on the subway train. His head lightened as he tried to recall his memories. He turned to George.

"It is ok, Josh," George reassured. "Just enjoy."

"Enjoy what?" Grabbing hold of either side of his chair time began to speed up around them.

Dusk formed then ebbed away into darkness as a bird's chorus became replaced by the distant hum of crickets. Josh followed the gentle curved rise of a crescent moon and its trail of moonbeams skipping across the lake in a tight white fan of light.

As the moon came to a gradual halt high above the temple on the hillside time slowed back down to its usual rate.

"What happened, why did we go faster?"

"There is so much to see," George replied. "It was just a way to get to the good parts."

"But, how is it possible?"

"Anything is possible here."

"Here?" Josh hoped that George could tell him where here was.

"Time has no meaning here, Josh, not as we perceive it anyway. For along this journey we can travel back and forth to anywhere or anywhen."

Staring around him, Josh found some comfort the young man and woman continued to laugh and giggle over their now candle lit table at the far end of the restaurant.

The staff cleared tables and swept the restaurant's wooden slat floor, it was late and they were ready for home. As the owner added up the check for his final customers of the day he called his daughter over, flicking the bill in the young couple's direction before handing it to her. Walking across the restaurant she placed it on their table and stood back head bowed in hope she had been subtle enough in her father's hint for them to leave.

On paying for the bill the relieved waitress shared a smile with the strange foreigners who had laughed all day and for most of the night. Seeing they had left a little money for her, she quickly pocketed the tip. On her return to the bar she thought of ways she could spend the extra money with her fellow colleague. She smiled to the young waiter who unbeknown to him had already gained her affections, although it would be a while before she would be admitting that to him.

The young woman looked to her watch. Showing the time to her new friend surprise spread across his face also. Had they really been here that long?

"What are they going to do now?" Josh asked George.

"Why do you ask?"

"Well it looks like they don't want to part company, like they want the night to go on forever," Josh watched the young couple as they stood and began to leave the restaurant.

Gesturing for her to leave first, the young woman thanked the young man for his courtesy and stepped down onto the street with a raised eyebrow and slight smile.

Josh began to stand.

"Leave them be awhile. We can always catch them up," George said. "If, that is what you really want to do."

"Of course I do. I want to know what happens next," Josh sat back down, still eager to follow the young couple as they disappeared into the night.

As the waiter and waitress smiled to each other and continued to clear the tables, Josh and George raised their feet as the waiter swept beneath them, unaware of the presence of his two extra customers.

"Why do you want to know what happens next?" George asked.

"I don't know. It's like I need to."

"But why?"

"Because they…"

"Because they glowed, Josh?"

"Yeah. That's it, they glowed. They really did," he realised that that was exactly what had happened. A kind of magic had circled and entwined around the young couple.

"You felt it as well then? Not everyone does, but to those who do it gives them something."

"Gives them what?"

"It gives them hope, only for a brief moment, yet that is all it takes."

"Hope for what, what's happening between these two?"

Not understanding the passion he felt of wanting to know the outcome of their encounter George looked to him.

"Do you feel full of energy? Are you invigorated by just being around them?"

George looked out into the street to where they had last seen the young couple.

"Josh, they are special. What we saw today was neither coincidence nor chance meeting. It was all about timing."

"Timing, but how?"

"Everything they have ever done, everywhere they have ever been, every decision they have ever made has brought them to today. To the precise moment they met here beside the banks of this beautiful lake." George pointed across the restaurant. "At that very table, Josh."

"But people meet every day, all over the world. What makes these two so special?"

"Because they are Noa Koo."

"Noa what?"

"Let me explain," George said, the chair's brittle wicker strips creaking beneath him as he leant back.

"The legend of the Noa Koo first originated in China many thousands of years ago," he began. "Long ago, before time had even been considered, there was a beautiful valley in the heart of China. Within that valley lived many people who were very different to those of today, for they lived happy and content and were neither male nor female, just one person who could reproduce on their own."

Josh settled back, his imagination caught as George continued.

"At one end of the valley stood a tall mountain. Amongst its snow-capped peaks high above the earth was a cave in which lived a dragon. Day after day the dragon would watch the people below him as they played and laughed. He became so jealous of their happiness that one day he swooped down through the valley and breathed a magical fire over each and every one of them. That fire caused the people's souls to leave their bodies. As the dragon watched those souls floated up into the sky before him, he then breathed another fiery spell over them, splitting each soul in half. Then, with a beat of his huge leathery wings he scattered these half souls across the world."

George paused. He glanced over to the moonlit lake and then back to Josh.

"In Asia they call these half souls Noa Koo, and believe that today everyone is looking for their own Noa Koo. So they can become whole once more as they were all those many years ago."

"Soul mates?"

"Yes, Josh. In the Western world they are called soul mates and here in Asia they go by the name of Noa Koo. Uniquely different words, yet they mean exactly the same thing, regardless of race, colour or gender. Because we are all equal, as equal as the day are souls were broken in two and scattered to the four corners of the earth."

"So that's what's happening to these two now. They're, ah, rejoining?"

"Yes they are. Although they do not recognize each other quite just yet, they can sense that something is happening to them."

"How can they not recognise each other? They're soul mates aren't they? Noa, ahh…"

"Noa Koo."

"Yeah, Noa Koo," Josh shifted in his chair.

25

"It does not always work like that. Imagine an old cup broken in half for many years. Somebody finds these two pieces and sees that they were once whole."

Josh watched George's hands, a piece of the imaginary cup in each.

"They fumble around until both fit back together again. Yet the pieces will not stay that way and soon fall apart."

"So they need a bond?"

"Exactly. With the cup it would need glue to bond and keep those two pieces together."

"But, with soul mates, what kind of bond do they need?"

"Time. They just need a little time."

"How long of a time?"

"Questions, questions," George laughed. "I am afraid I cannot answer that one, for who can? It could be minutes, hours, days or even years. But they will get there in the end."

"In the end?"

"Yes, Josh, in the end. You see everyone meets their Noa Koo at least once in their lifetime. Sometimes that very person they have been looking for is there already, right in front of their eyes. It just takes some a while to recognise them."

"But, what if they don't see it, what if they don't recognise each other?"

"Oh, no need to worry about that. Destiny, kismet, synchronicity, call it what you will, these factors will simply not leave them be."

Josh looked back to the table where the young couple had sat.

"Josh, now that they have finally met the games afoot so to say and the wheels of fate have been set in motion. They will experience pushes and nudges in the right direction until they are reunited again and again. Until their bond is complete and they become whole once more."

Josh knew of the theories on fate and destiny, but had never considered it before. Warmed by George's explanation his thoughts returned to the young couple.

"Come on," George stood. "Let us catch them up."

Together they left the restaurant, Josh laughing as George jumped down the stone steps like an excited child, as keen as he to retrace the young couple's steps back to the main street.

Walking beneath dim street lamps casting an eerie shadow over the market's now empty trestle tables, Josh looked to the hungry dogs below them. They growled and picked nervously at scraps of food left over after a busy days trading.

Ignoring their bickering yelps, Josh stared up to the moon high above the temple surrounded by flickering stars in a warm Asian night sky.

"Look," George whispered beside him.

Following his gaze towards the lake, Josh saw the silhouette of the young man and woman standing against its shimmering waters.

CHAPTER SIX

Fascinated by the young man and woman standing before the lake, Josh sensed the overwhelming want of contact between them both. The two moved closer until almost touching.

In silence the young man moved closer. Her eyes still locked on his, the young woman followed his lead. Inches from each other they paused. Both jumped back, shocked by the noise from across the street. Josh jumped with them. Over discarded bones and off cuts of brown meat a fight had broken out between the dogs behind him and George. The young couple laughed nervously to the affray then to each other as they left the lake's banks.

Returning to the road Josh and George kept their distance as they followed the two onto the main street, leaving the dogs behind to continue their free meal.

Walking deep in conversation past neon signs buzzing above closed restaurants doors, the young woman came to a stop at the entrance of an alleyway.

"Well, this is me," she said to the young man.

"Will you be ok from here?"

The young woman looked down the dark walkway and to her guesthouse at its end.

"Yeah, I'll be fine." She hesitated and looked up to him. "Anyway, it was nice meeting you."

"You too," he hovered for a moment. "Good night," he turned from her and continued alone towards his own guesthouse.

The young woman watched him walk away.

"Hey," she called out to him.

The young man swung back round.

"I know it's late, but do you want to maybe, hang out a bit more?"

"That would be good," his face lit up as he walked back to her. "I don't think I can sleep much anyhow."

"Neither do I," she whispered to herself, delving into her bag for her keys.

George watched Josh engrossed in the scene before him. Josh turned to him.

"What?"

"Oh, nothing," George said. "Want to see more?"

Josh's eyebrows rose.

"I will take that as a yes," George guided the way down the dark alleyway and through the large rusty gates leading to the young woman's guesthouse.

Following them across a tree lined courtyard a sleeping security guard woke with a start. He jumped to his feet then relaxed on recognising the young woman.

"Namaste," he smiled to her.

"Namaste," the young couple replied together, finding comfort in their synchronicity and entering through the guesthouse's white paint flaked doors.

Watching them climb the guesthouse's set of concrete stairs, Josh and George slipped by the security guard unnoticed as he returned to his chair, lowered the peak of his cap and fell back to sleep.

After three flights they found the young man and woman halfway down a long corridor. Stood in front of a rickety wooden door the young woman opened the large padlock on its handle.

"I won't be a second," she said and disappeared into her room.

The young man waited patiently outside. She soon reappeared in a large knitted jumper.

"There you go," she passed him a jumper also and closed the padlock with a snap. "It's up here," she whispered to him and raced up another flight of stairs at the end of the corridor. The young man took after her, his two silent observers in tow.

The staircase led to an open doorway leading out onto the guesthouse's rooftop.

"Over here," the young woman called from the centre of the flat rooftop, each of them glad of their jumper's warmth in the nights slight chill.

Arranging two plastic chairs side by side with two before them for their feet to rest upon, they smiled to one another as they sat down and looked around them.

"Josh," George called from a wooden bench opposite. Josh sat down beside him and together they watched the young couple submersed in the moonlight's silver glow.

The young woman's finger panned across the Milky Way's pasty white line dissecting a clear, crisp sky in half. Josh followed her trail across the stars. Looking back to the young couple they took sips from the water bottle between them, their eyes never leaving the other's for a moment.

"They're starting to realise aren't they?" Josh said.

"And quickly."

"Is that normal?'

"It all depends, Josh. Some are quicker than others, but for these two the time is right. They are open and ready. Being themselves and accepting all around them."

Josh turned to George as the stars began to move.

"Again?"

"Only a few hours, Josh," George said as time sped up around them once more.

Like the hands of a clock the shadows of washing line poles swept over the rooftop. They bent and rose over the young couple, both unaware of the dark lines racing across their bodies. Stars faded as the sky decreased into a canvas of light blue and blended into a horizon of pure white of. As time resumed its usual pace the young couple sat together in silence, transfixed by the landscape in the distance.

Unmasked by the night sky, a large mountain range had appeared before them. Spread across the town's northern side, snow-capped peaks glowed pink in early morning sunlight, casting a harsh contrast where ice met with granite. Their view not leaving its beauty, the young couple both reached down for the bottle of water between them. Josh cringed as their heads knocked together with a dull thud.

Recoiling in tired surprise, the young couple both rubbed their foreheads. They looked to each other and began to laugh. The young woman's laughter faded as she leant forwards and touched the red mark below the young man's hairline. Looking deep into her dark brown eyes he mirrored her tender actions. She felt his inquisitive fingertips trace across her temple and stroked down her cheek's soft skin. Moving closer their eyes closed as they bridged the gap between them. Cautious at first, they kissed for a brief moment as if they had for years or even lifetimes before. Gently breaking away they looked to each other with pleasure and disbelief at what they had felt.

The young couple rose from their seats in silence, their hands slipping into one another's as they walked across the rooftop to the doorway entered hours earlier. As they disappeared down the stairs George looked at Josh.

"Are you all right, Josh?"

"Yes, it's just that."

"Yes, Josh?"

"That kiss, it seemed so…"

"Familiar?"

"Yeah. Not so much a memory, but…"

"Recognisable?"

"Yeah that's it, recognisable." He turned to George. "Why?"

George glanced to the doorway then back to him.

"Often when we witness strong emotions played out between others they trigger powerful feelings hidden deep within us, bringing our subconscious thoughts and memories to the fore."

Josh nodded. He had felt something unlock inside him. The young couple's kiss and gentle caresses had given him a brief glimpse of hope, filling him with great warmth and security. The recognition of these Noa Koo who had now found and begun to identify each other puzzled him. As did the slight twinge of loss now felt. George sensed his loss.

"Do not worry Josh, it will come again. When those hidden emotions have been experienced once, the doors have been opened and those feelings will be able to return again. As long that is, we keep our thoughts open."

"If it happens once, then it can happen again?"

"Yes, it is just a case of knowing those emotions of love and hope are there within us all in the first place. Then the rest is easy."

George rose to his feet and clapped his hands.

"Right, time to move on."

Josh rushed ahead towards the stairs ready to see what was going to happen next.

"Oh, no, Josh," George called out to him. "We are going a different way. It may be more comfortable if you look to the floor."

Josh did as George suggested, but not before he saw the world around him blur into a swirl of pinks and blues.

Shiny white tiles replaced the dusty rooftop below him. Staring up to a ceiling of metal and glass he looked around the large building he and George now found themselves in.

A shrill voice rang through the air and as people passed by with suitcases Josh knew he was in an airport.

CHAPTER SEVEN

Josh steadied himself as he and George looked to the airport's entrance. Armed guards admitted two familiar figures through its doors.

The young man and woman trudged towards the ticket desk. Each carried large backpacks strapped to them, as well as solemn looks.

"What's happened?"

"She is leaving, Josh."

"She's leaving? He is too right? I mean, he's got all his things with him."

"Let us see shall we?"

George walked across the main hall to the young couple and leant beside them over a ticket desk's counter.

"Want to change," the young man said.

Holding his airline ticket out to the woman behind the counter she looked to the ticket and then back to him. Trying once more with his request the ticket clerk finally understood. She pointed to a large building opposite the airport.

Turning to the young woman, the young man dropped his backpack to the floor and kissed her once.

"I won't be long," he said. He looked up to the flight schedule board above them and then his watch before running to the main entrance and its guards, passport and ticket held tight in his hand.

The young woman smiled across the counter and looked to her own air ticket. Leaning over her shoulder Josh read it with her. She had a twenty four layover in Mumbai, India, before flying on to New York City's JFK airport, and home.

Glancing nervously at her watch, fifteen minutes dragged by with still no sign of her love.

"Is he going to make it?" Josh asked.

George gave no answer as the young woman's eyes fixed anxiously on the flight times board above her.

"Josh," George said. "Look."

The young man vaulted from the adjacent building and into the arms of the airport guards. They checked his details twice before letting him re-enter the airport's main hall. He raced over to the young woman, a huge smile upon him.

"I got it," he held his new ticket high above his head. "I got it changed, I'm coming with you."

The young woman hugged him.

"Come on," she said. "We've only got twenty minutes to check in."

Helping each other with their packs they hurried to the check in desk, Josh and George following close behind them.

The queue was long and the young couple planned their twenty four hour visit to India.

"I can't believe you changed your ticket," the young woman said.

The young man grabbed her round the waist and pulled her close.

"Yeah?" He gave a boyish grin. "I just wanted to spend another day with you."

Wrapping her arms around him they kissed.

"Next," the woman behind the check in desk called. "Next," she called again, breaking the young man and woman apart.

"Sorry," the young woman said when greeted by a stern look.

Placing her backpack beside the desk she handed over her passport and ticket. The check in woman scrutinised the young woman's passport before handing it back to her with a boarding card tucked inside.

"Next."

The young man handed over his passport and new ticket. The check in woman leafed through his passport three times before glaring up at him.

"What?" The young man shrugged.

Leaving her seat without a word she walked over to her manager and handed the young man's passport to him. He studied it several times before approaching the young couple.

"No," he said, thrusting the passport back to the young man.

"Huh?" The young couple replied, confused by this turn of events.

"No, you cannot fly."

"Why not?"

"You have no visa for India."

"But I'm only there for twenty four hours. They changed my ticket. They said it would be ok," the young man pointed to the building beyond the entrance doors.

Taking the passport off him and roughly flicking through its pages once more, the manger handed it back to the young man again.

"No," he shook his head and walked away as a security guard stepped forward and ushered the young man from the queue.

Tears welled in the young man's eyes, and Josh watched on as the young couple hugged.

"Shhh, I know, and I've only just found you," the young woman whispered, their warm tears combining on her cheek. They couldn't believe it. In seconds their plans had all been brought to a halt. The young woman glared at the airport's speakers announcing her flight.

"I have to go," she said.

The young man stared at her then to the escalators that would take her onwards towards home.

"I know," he whispered back as hand in hand they walked to the foot of the moving staircase in silence.

Embracing for a final time, the young woman stroked his cheek as she stepped onto the escalator. She looked to him.

"Goodbye," she said before disappearing from view.

Hovering on the spot where they had last held one another, the young man picked up his bag and slumped down onto one of the empty seats next to him.

"Why?" Josh looked at the young man now sat despondent, his head cupped in his hands.

"This is sometimes the way of things, Josh," George replied. "But, you must remember, they have spent a fantastic three weeks together. A time filled with love and laughter."

"But why can't that continue? It doesn't seem fair."

"You cannot stay on top all the time. There would simply be no balance in the world if that were true. When times are good you have to grasp them and enjoy them to the fullest, because eventually things will and do turn around. But, Josh, the trick is to remember that when bad times are with you, good times are only around the corner, waiting just for you to experience joy once more."

George looked over to the young man and then back to Josh.

"Josh, the sun invariably does, and will always shine again."

The young man jumped from his seat and ran past Josh and George towards the escalator. As his foot hammered down onto its second metal step he flew backwards as a security guard pulled him back from the moving stairway.

The guard had followed the young couple from the check in desk and had watched them unnoticed from behind one of the airport's red brick pillars. With no time for protest he escorted the young man and his backpack across the airport and through its exit doors.

From outside the young man glared at the guard through the airport's glass doors and began to complain. He stopped on noticing the armed guards beside him toying with the guns strapped around their necks. He fell silent. Deciding now was not the best time for confrontation he sat down on his backpack.

"Ready, Josh?" George said.

"Ready for what? To go?"

George pointed to the set of fire doors next to the ticket desk.

"But what's going on?" Josh called out to George already half way to the exit doors. "Why was he so determined to get back to her?"

With last glance to the young man he caught up with George.

"I mean, I can understand one last goodbye, but he was possessed."

By George's expression Josh saw there would be no answers. Not just yet at least.

"Will he be ok?"

"He will be fine," George shoved the metal bar across the airport's heavy fire doors.

Those doors flew open to reveal a dark passageway. The subway's platform and their train waited for them at its end.

To Josh it was quite a shock to leave the airports clean environment and walk into the tunnel. Deep down he knew it was time for them to leave this place, to move forward into the unknown and onto their next stop. Together they walked down the corridor and boarded the train. The carriage doors closed behind them.

"I suppose you would like to know what happened back there," George said, as they took their seats and the train left the station.

"Of course I do."

George leant back and looked to Josh.

"They followed their hearts, Josh. They let go of all they knew and put their trust within one another."

"But," Josh protested.

"They both followed their dreams to find out all that they can be. And while they were doing just that they found each other again."

Thinking back to the restaurant where the young couple had first met, Josh remembered the rooftop and then the young man now sat alone outside the airport.

"Why did he rush back to her like that?" He asked.

"Because there was one thing they forgot to share with each other."

Josh couldn't imagine a thing the young couple had not shared during their time together.

"And what was that?"

"They forgot to exchange addresses and phone numbers."

Josh now understood why the young man had dashed back to her.

"All they have left now," George said, his view not leaving the end of the subway car. "Is a name and a city."

CHAPTER EIGHT

Although soothed in the subway train's warmth and gentle sway Josh's thoughts filled with the young couple. The image of the young man sat alone outside the airport haunted him.

"Ready for your next stop?" George asked.

Wanting to ask of the young couple's fate he instead just nodded as George rose to his feet.

The train slowed and rumbled into the station of their second stop. Staring through the windows to the hordes of people on its platform the train's doors slid open. Josh saw not one of them tried to enter the train.

A commuter looked up from his newspaper and along the platform in impatience for his next ride.

"They can't see us can they?" Josh whispered.

"No, they cannot," George stepped into the crowd. He looked back at Josh. "Ready?"

Edging out of the train he tried his best not to nudge the people around him.

George led the way down busy corridors and up flights of stairs.

"This way," he pointed to one of three long escalators. Stepping onto grilled steps they travelled upwards. Josh gasped on reaching the top.

A vast crowded hall spread out before them. Josh looked across its teeming marbled floors to the three tall arched windows opposite. The windows cast huge shafts of light onto the people below before they delved back into the shadows. Weaving around each other as if in a highly trained dance troop, not one commuter touched another beneath a painted ceiling of zodiac constellations and gilded stars.

"Josh," George nodded towards an information booth, its four-sided brass clock stood high in the centre of the main concourse. To Josh it seemed an oasis of calm in this sea of people.

Sidestepping and waltzing between the crowds, Josh partnered dozens of people without their knowledge until an old woman in layers of tattered clothing stopped in front of him. With all his newly acquainted footwork skills he couldn't avoid crashing into her.

"Hey, what's your problem?" She said.

Josh looked behind him.

"Hey," the old woman's grimy lined face contorted. "I'm talking to you," she jabbed a dirty finger at Josh.

"You can see me?" He said.

"Of course I can, what's wrong with you? Are you crazy?"

An overweight businessman puffed his way towards them and Josh turned to speak to him. He knocked Josh aside, unaware of his presence.

"Honey," the old woman said. "You gotta be careful round here, it ain't safe, they're everywhere you know."

"Who? Who's everywhere?"

The old woman looked so pleased someone had took an interest in what she had to say that Josh wondered how many people simply dismissed her and walked away. She leant forwards and whispered to him.

"People. People like you."

"Like me?"

"Yes, people like you who think that no one can see them."

Her eyes darted around the station. She moved closer to Josh.

"I see them though," she whispered. "I see them all the time."

Josh nodded and looked over to George.

"Yes, and I can see your friend too."

The old woman waved to George who smiled and waved back to her from the information booth. Her face lit up.

"I see him here all the time," she waved once more, her collection of bags rustling around her wrist.

Seeing a twinkle in the woman's eye, Josh realised she was not as old as he had first thought. He even considered that in her younger days she had probably been quite beautiful, seeing her in a different light as she enjoyed her moment of interaction with George. Josh also wondered if at one time she might have had a home, a family, a job, or even been part of a community. He couldn't understand how she had ended up this way.

"Ahh, he's lovely," the old woman continued to look over to George. "He always says hello."

George beckoned Josh to him.

"I have to go now," he said to the old woman.

Her moment of joy dimmed.

"That's ok," she said. "They all leave in the end."

She looked to the floor and then back up to him.

"Hey, can you spare a dollar?" She patted her stomach. Josh reached into his pockets. He remembered his missing wallet.

"Ahh, go on," she said. "Look again."

Josh searched his pockets once more for the old woman's benefit. He looked back at her in surprise. From his jacket pocket he pulled out three notes. The old woman stared at the twenty, fifty and one hundred dollar bill in his hand. Josh hesitated. How could he have missed this money before?

The old woman continued to eye his newfound treasure.

Trying to figure out which of the bills to give her, Josh paused and the remembered George's words about not needing any money on his journey. He handed over all three bills.

The old woman gasped and cupped Josh's face in her hands.

"Thank you," she said, the once harsh tone in her voice gone.

Pocketing the money, she waved to George once more and turned to Josh. She winked to him before melting back into the crowds.

Josh felt content. He had given and taken nothing in return, yet now he felt like the richest man on earth. It was then Josh realised his real wealth lay in the knowledge and experiences he was now undergoing with George on his journey. Could giving always feel like this? With this thought he waded through the crowds.

"You met Abby then?" George greeted him.

Josh had not even considered she had a name and he looked for her. Although the information booth gave a good view of the hall and its people he could not find her. Feeling some sadness from their encounter, he tried to balance this with the contradiction of the happiness felt from giving.

"She is special, Josh, this is why she can see us."

"Special? How can she be special?"

"Abby may not be in the most ideal situation. Outcaste and on the fringes of society, but, she is free. Free from all constraints and conformities, totally open to the world around her. This is why she is special. This is how she can see what most do not."

With some guilt, Josh recalled how he had seen her so differently when she had waved to George.

"What happened to her?" How did she end up like this, she couldn't have always been this way, could she?"

"No, Abby has not always been this way. But, she made her choices."

"They couldn't have been very good ones."

George shook his head.

"It was not a bad choice Abby or anyone else made for her Josh. She is exactly where she should be at this present moment in time. It was a choice that led her to her current situation. But, by no means was it a bad one."

Josh looked for Abby again through the crowds to no avail.

"You see, Josh, there is no such thing as a bad choice or wrong decision. For every choice we make leads us onto where we should be going, onto the next chapter in our life. No matter how bad that chapter may seem at the time."

"But how can Abby's situation possibly be right? She's on the street. Homeless."

"Josh, sometimes people have to fall."

"Why?"

"Why? So they can get back up again."

"So will she. Abby. Will she get back up again?"

"She will get there. Everybody does in the end. I do not know when or where it will be, but she has what it takes to do so."

George's words gave Josh fresh hope for the old woman.

"There is one other factor to remember though," George leant towards him. "I did not say that people only fall once."

His words shocked Josh. He hadn't considered you could fall again, once seemed awful enough.

"That though is Abby's path. Not yours, not mine or anybody else's, just hers. Do not worry so much. Smile, everything is happening as it should."

Josh looked to the people milling past him. Some held cell phones snug against ear and cheek whilst others rushed by in silence, desperate to break free of the throng.

"See anyone you know?" George asked.

Surprised by the question, Josh shook his head.

"No."

"Look closer, Josh."

There was a disturbance four or five people deep in the drift of bodies before him. A sole individual rushed against the flow of the crowd and carved a distinct path between the people leaving a small gap in their wake. George made for the opening.

"Who is it?" Josh called.

Giving no answer, George continued his pursuit of the lone figure. Following behind Josh saw every person George squeezed by became calmer, leaving a trail of smiling faces and bemused looks to why they suddenly felt happier and more hopeful for the day ahead.

The crowds lessened as they approached an alcove set back in the walls of the hall. Josh caught sight of who they had chased.

"Is that him?" He said. "But his hair, it's much longer."

George nodded.

"Six months have passed since we left him outside those airport doors."

The young man dived into one of the two alcove entrances and Josh began to follow.

"There is no need to follow him in there," George pointed up to the sign above the bathroom's door. "He will not be long."

CHAPTER NINE

Waiting for the young man to reappear, a man and woman laughed and flirted beside the entrance of the alcove. George pointed them out to Josh.

Guessing them to be employees on a break Josh looked to the poster behind them and its cartoon drawing of a fat jovial ticket collector dressed the same as they. The fat man's arm stretched out and gestured to a picture of a large lake where a train wound its way along its banks amid trees of red, gold and bright orange.

The man and women continued to laugh in front of the picturesque scene. George watched Josh for a reaction from him. Taking no interest in the pair, Josh looked back to the alcove and breathed in enticing smells of a coffee stand a few feet away, almost tasting its thick rich aroma in the air.

"Look," George said.

The young man emerged from the bathroom. Head bowed, he fumbled with the buttons of his jeans unaware he headed towards the door opposite, and its constant flow of women. Josh and George looked on as the inevitable happened and the young man bumped into one of them. Raising his head he began to apologise. He stopped. Josh saw who it was he had stumbled into. Her red hair was unmistakable.

The young man and women stared at each other. Looking up at him she tucked a stray strand of hair behind one ear.

"Hey, how are you?" The young man spoke first.

"Good." She nodded coyly, her lower lip clenched between her teeth.

"What are you doing here?" They said at the same time, only to laugh nervously at their synchronicity.

Josh felt relief in that laughter. Even though a hint of awkwardness lingered, something else was present too. A sense of belonging remained between the young couple. It circled them hungrily, growing stronger by the second.

"Well that was a coincidence," Josh said.

"There are no coincidences happening here," George replied.

The young woman began to giggle. One hand covered her mouth as she pointed down to the young man's jeans. He blushed and buttoned himself up.

"So they're back together now?" Josh said. "They don't seem to have lost anything at all. Even after all this time."

"Not necessarily." George shook his head. He saw Josh's disappointment. "Remember how I said that from the moment they first met the wheels of fate had been set in motion?"

Josh watched the young man and woman as they talked together.

"They have been within that wheel of fate for the last six months." George continued. "At rest in its hub."

"It's hub?"

"Where the wheels momentum moves much slower, allowing them some peace and time. Yet they cannot remain in its centre forever. The wheel is ever moving, they cannot fight its constant spinning. Eventually at some point they will be forced out onto its edges where the spinning is faster. More vigorous."

"And this is one of those moments?"

"Yes, Josh," George smiled over at the young man and woman. "This is one of those very moments."

As the young man and woman continued to talk, Josh sensed a want of touch between them once more.

"Now they are on its outer rim," George said. "Turning faster and faster. It is up to them what happens next."

"But what happens if they don't take this opportunity?"

"Then they will simply return to the calmness in the centre of the wheel. But remember, if they choose to return to the hub once more there is one overriding factor."

"And what's that?"

"As I said before, the wheel is ever turning. They will both be flung out onto its outer rim time and time again until…"

"Until what?"

"Until they walk the path they are meant to be on. Together, side by side. They are Noa Koo after all."

Another young woman approached the young couple and took hold of her friends arm.

"Come on," she said to the young woman. "We're going to be late." She turned to the young man.

"Hello, nice to meet you, I'm sorry we've really got to go."

Pulling the young woman away, the young man watched on helplessly as his love looked to him. She smiled once before becoming devoured by the crowds.

Reaching up onto his toes the young man looked for her amongst the mass of people.

"Not again," Josh said.

"No, look. He has spotted her," George said as the young man raced to her.

Trying to force his way through the crowds, they proved too busy for the young man. Defeated from reaching her, he watched her slip out of sight beneath a low archway with golden letters emblazoned across its top. The young man stood still, buffeted by passersby unaware of his loss.

It had all happened so quickly. One moment she had been there in his grasp only to be taken away from him again. The pain and longing he had tried to push away over the last six months resurfaced in seconds. He turned and headed straight for Josh and George.

"Can he see us?" Josh saw the intensity the young man's eyes held as he marched towards them.

"No, Josh," George gently nudged him aside.

The young man breezed between them, as unconscious of their existence as everyone else. Wrapped up within his own thoughts he made his way to the exit at the far side of the hall, determined that this time nothing would bar his way.

George began to follow him.

"Coming, Josh?" He called over his shoulder.

Following the young man out of the train station, down a flight of stone steps and into bright sunlight, the young man's pace slowed and Josh took a moment to look around.

A busy street swarmed with traffic and people, and tall buildings rose high in all directions against brilliant blue skies. Josh turned to the building they had just left. Stepping back into the street he stared up at the sculptured figures in its eaves. George pulled him back as a car raced by in a yellow blur.

"Thank you." Josh glanced back to the taxicab.

George nodded up the street where the young man walked ahead deep in contemplation. Turning left one block ahead, Josh and George followed behind him. Gliding through the morning rush of people they soon entered a quieter stretch of road.

"I can't believe he lost her again," Josh said.

"The patterns and clues where there laid out before him."

"What patterns? What clues?"

"They were there no matter how slight they may have appeared. Did you notice any?"

"Well, there was the young man, the young woman. They met and it ended with someone coming along and stopping him from being able to get to her again."

"That was the pattern, now, where were the clues?"

"The train station?"

"Think back to our first stop. What was the young man doing when they first met?"

"Writing?"

"Yes he was, but there was something else."

"Drinking coffee?"

George nodded.

"Drinking coffee? How can that be a clue?"

"This is their story, Josh, special to them. Believe it or not, coffee does play an important role along their paths."

Not understanding how something so trivial could be so important, he then remembered the train station and the coffee stand next to where the young couple had met once more. It all started to become clearer as Josh recalled the station's staff, and how they had flirted together beside the large poster of a lake.

"The two workers," he said. "By the poster."

"Often, if ever, we do not see the clues around us until later. Much later when we look back on certain times in our lives. If we can see a pattern unfolding in our lives and spot the clues before us, then we can sometimes piece it all together and maybe perceive the outcome."

"Like telling the future?"

"Nearly, but not quite. Think it simply as a highly developed sense of intuition. Small hints along the way to what may or may not happen, all as different and unique as each and every one of us."

George watched the young man continue to walk ahead.

"Josh, it is recognising these clues that appear before us, that is the key to it all. Everyone can do it. They just have to be aware those clues are there in the first place. Once they do then all will become more and more apparent to them."

"So when she left for the staircase, had he seen a pattern emerging and noticed the clues around him, he may have been able to foretell his path would be blocked to her again?"

"Exactly," George smiled. "Also, had he noticed the combination of coffee, the flirting staff, and the lake, he may have had an idea that they were soon to meet again."

"And this time he may have got her phone number."

A motorbike roared past them. It raced through the quiet street as Josh turned his attention to the young man.

Ambling on ahead head bowed he stepped out into the street.

The young man broke free from his thoughts as the speeding motorbike headed towards him. Swerving hard its wing mirror deflected off the young man's arm sending both him and rider crashing to the floor.

Tucking himself into a ball the rider rolled down the street as the young man was tossed sideways. His head met the floor with a bump.

Looking at his lifeless body Josh vaulted over to him and stared down to the red streaks covering the young man's face and torso.

CHAPTER TEN

The motorbike screamed, its rear wheel spinning close to the young man's feet. The rider checked himself over and turned the machine off. He looked down at the young man and then to the three large flat boxes on the floor beside him. He picked them up as the young man groaned and tasted the red streak running across his mouth.

"Ahh no, my boss is going to kill me," the motorbike rider yelled. "You're gonna have to pay for this, buddy."

Throwing the dented pizza boxes to the floor the young man lifted up onto his elbows. Looking down to the strips of cheese on his clothes he tasted the rich tomato sauce on his lips once more.

A siren whooped once as a police car came to a halt next to them. Two officers jumped from its doors, one went to subdue the irate pizza deliveryman whilst the other rushed over to the young man.

"Are you all right?" The policewoman asked.

"I think so."

She hid her smile as the young man picked an anchovy from his hair.

"Hey lady, he's got to pay for all this. He's going to pay," the rider whined behind her.

"Quiet," she shouted at him.

He stopped and glared at the young man.

"Don't you worry about him," the policewoman said. "You seem ok to me. There's a hospital near here, we'll give you a ride and get you checked out properly."

Helping the young man to his feet and into the patrol car she pointed at the motorbike rider.

"You." She said. "Stay here, we won't be long."

Slamming her door the policewoman looked from its window.

"I mean it," she growled at him before driving away.

Kicking his bike, the deliveryman looked to the departing police car then kicked his bike again. George walked to him. Placing a hand on his shoulder the man began to smile. As George released his grip the rider picked up his bike, moved it to the side of the road and waited for the police to return.

"I think I know which hospital she means," Josh said.

"You do?"

"Yeah. How do I know?"

"Lead the way."

Josh somehow knew that would be George's only reply.

Crossing streets and avenues they passed the police car entwined within the city's busy traffic.

Not understanding how he knew his way through this labyrinth of roads Josh wondered if his memory was returning as the hospital came into view.

The hospital's chaotic waiting room made the outside streets seem serene. With all seats occupied people lined its walls. Security guards watched over the awaiting patients who either bickered with the nurses on duty or amongst themselves, and doctors looked to sheets of x-rays whilst barking orders to the young interns following them.

"There," Josh pointed across the room to the two police officers. They had left the young man in a wheel chair who was now being wheeled past the guards through a security door.

"Better be quick, Josh," George said.

Racing across the waiting room Josh bounced off a bewildered doctor sending a pile of x-rays high in the air. With the door closing Josh slid through its gap.

"That was close," he said as the door slammed shut behind him.

George waved to him through the doors small window from the other side. Motioning Josh to continue on alone Josh nodded back to him and walked into the treatment room.

Loops of pale blue curtain jutted out from the walls on either side of the room. Josh knew the young man was behind one of them. The question was, which one?

Beginning with the cubicle next to him, he tried three others until finding the young man laying fully clothed on a bed propped up by several pillows. Josh slipped between the curtains.

Footsteps approached the cubicle. The curtain pulled back with one clean sweep. Both Josh and the young man stared at the five people stood at the foot of his bed.

Two interns flanked a tall senior doctor and a nurse stood either side of them. One of the nurses looked as if in shock.

"Somebody smells good," one of the junior doctors sniggered.

His senior doctor shot him a terse stare and gestured to the other for a diagnosis. The intern poked, prodded and questioned the young man as the senior doctor listened to his student's analysis.

"Right, you're free to go," the doctor said. He pointed at the young red headed nurse. "You. Get him cleaned up."

The doctor leered at the other nurse before moving his entourage onto the next cubicle.

Anger flushed across the nurse's face. Her expression was soon replaced by concern as she rushed over to the young man.

"What happened to you?" She asked.

The young man couldn't believe it. They had met twice in one day, in one hour. Josh was also stunned. If only George could see this, he thought. He smiled to himself. Yes, he probably knew already.

Leaning over the young man, both he and the young woman were lost for words. The senior doctor coughed and stared at them from the next cubicle. Glaring at him, she drew the curtain between them happy to deal with any consequences later. Returning to the young man he began to speak. She placed a finger on his lips.

"Shhh," she took a cloth and began to clean his face with slow delicate strokes.

The warm fabric turned red as she drew it softly from behind his ear to the nape of his neck. The young man looked up to her in silence. On occasion their eyes would meet and she would smile to him before returning to her work.

A light sensation captured them both. They inhaled each other's chemistry, their molecules held in recognition from life times past, weaving and dancing together until reforming into one entity. The young woman leant closer. His dark hair shone as she worked the cloth across his hairline. As her breath played feather light upon his brow their eyes met once more.

"Namaste," she whispered to him. "I missed you," her lips brushed against his.

"Namaste," the young man responded with soft pressure, home again.

Josh watched the unconditional love flow between them. Also becoming light headed he leant back onto a table of chrome dishes. The ring of metal on tiled flooring caused the young couple to break free. They stared at the empty space where Josh stood.

Feeling terrible he had disturbed their moment the curtains flailed back.

"What's going on here?" The senior doctor shouted.

His two interns grinned behind him and the young woman gave both a fierce glare.

"You should have finished up here by now. Clear this mess up," he stared down to the chrome dishes and stormed off.

The other nurse stared at the young woman, her eyes wide. Josh recognised her from the train station.

The young woman looked to her Noa Koo. How could she leave him now?

"Nurse," the doctor yelled.

Picking up the dishes she turned to the young man.

"Outpatients," she winked, and then was gone.

Watching her leave he rolled off the bed and made for the outpatient's clinic, unaware Josh walked at his side down.

Charging ahead the young man's arms stretched out and he pushed the clinic's doors open. Walking through them together, Josh saw George wave to him from across the room between the doors of two elevators. Joining him the young man sat down in front of them.

Josh told George of the young couple's reunion.

"See Josh, although they both did not know it, they were still reeling from their last encounter. Those wheels of fate spun so fast their momentum simply carried them on to meet again."

"So soon?"

"Imagine two magnets locked together. As you pull them apart, the bonds keeping them there begin to diminish. The attraction is gone and nothing remains. But, Josh, if the pull between them stays close, the invisible forces holding them in place linger and it is harder to stop the magnets from snapping back together again."

"It's been what, less than an hour?" Josh began to understand. "So the bonds between the young couple where still strong?"

George nodded.

"So they are ready now? This is it?"

"That is still up to them."

Josh showed his disappointment once more.

"Sometimes, when fate races ahead this fast and its participants are still not headed in the same direction, then they will certainly be dragged towards it, like or not."

"But, you said destiny won't let them be."

"Wait and see, my friend," George smiled. "Wait and see."

Josh looked over to the young man and the elderly homeless man now sat beside him. A tattered baseball cap rested on a head of matted hair which blended into an unkempt beard. The homeless man leant over and sniffed the young man.

"Hey, mister," he said. "You taste as good as you smell?"

The young man shifted in his seat as the old man's nose crinkled and he tried to take a bite from the young man's shoulder.

"You still hungry, Arthur?"

The old man stopped, his jaws wide open. Both he and the young man looked up to the voice.

"I think it's time for you to leave," the young woman smiled.

Giving her a toothless grin and without any fuss, the old man made his way to the exit where he waved goodbye before waddling out of sight.

"Every day he comes here," the young woman said. "We feed him, but most days he tries to take a nibble out of someone. Today it was you. Feel special?"

"Very," the young man said as his Noa Koo smiled down at him.

The senior doctor reappeared with his troop close behind him.

"Right, so what have we learnt so far?" He asked.

Seeing the young woman had broken free of the group he sauntered over to her.

"This is not exactly what I meant by after patient care, nurse," he smiled to the others.

His treatment of nurses had always been the same. Unless that was he had taken an interest in one of them.

"Why can't you be as wonderful as this young lady here?" He gestured to the other nurse. She swooned and began to blush.

The young woman couldn't believe her colleague and best friend held an attraction to this awful man.

"Oh my, God," the young woman said to her friend. "I can't

believe you're falling for his rubbish."

The entire room fell silent.

Looking to the young woman with fresh respect the two junior doctors couldn't contain their laughter. They knew of the senior doctor's reputation with young student nurses. They also knew of his expensive wife and their two equally spoilt children.

The other nurse began to giggle. She knew what her friend was like.

"I can't believe you," she mouthed silently to her.

"You." The doctor shouted. "Get out of my sight."

Tears began to well in the young woman's eyes. The young man saw the strength she held in not letting the doctor see them fall.

"It's ok," she said. "I'm gone already."

The whole room watched her walk to one of the elevator's open doors.

"That's my girl," the young man said diving after her.

Arms folded at the back of the elevator the young woman watched him barge past the doctor as its doors began to slide together.

"Come on," she whispered. "Come on."

Bouncing off a large coffee machine, its quarters bled onto the floor behind him as he slid between closing doors and into the young woman's arms.

The young couple never heard the applause of the outpatient's room, or see the senior doctor's deserved humiliation. Nor would they ever know the hope they had given to so many people that day.

As the second elevator's doors opened Josh and George entered alone and descended.

It was of little surprise to Josh when the doors opened to reveal their subway car ahead.

CHAPTER ELEVEN

"How do you feel?"

The subway car hummed and swayed around Josh. He had become to view the subway car as a comforting respite between stops made. Lost in the setting George's words did not register.

"How do you feel?" George asked again.

The train jolted once, dragging Josh from his meditative state.

"I'm not sure," he replied.

Wrapped up in the young couple's story he hadn't considered his own feelings. George used his silence to gently coax Josh to continue.

"I hadn't thought about it, how I was feeling," Josh said. "I guess I've been just going with the flow."

"Going with the flow," George smiled. "I have always enjoyed that expression."

"I mean, I've been…"

"Living in the present moment?"

George's words struck Josh. He realised that was what he had been doing all along. With no thoughts of the little past he could remember or towards an unknown future, he had just been in the present moment. What shocked Josh was that he had done so unconsciously with George's guidance, letting him discover it on his own. Now it would never be lost to him.

Witnessing the sparks of awareness begin to flourish within Josh, George knew his doors of awakening had opened never to be closed to him again.

A crucial part of Josh's puzzle had clicked into place, a piece that would act as a bridge to many other revelations. Like a child having mastered its first steps the impulse to run overwhelmed him.

"Show me more," he said.

George saw the want in his eyes.

"The rest will come. Think what you have learnt, contemplate on only that. This will open up new avenues to you towards other lessons and answers."

"Answers? What answers?"

"Small steps, Josh, small steps. The answers from all life's lessons allow us to understand how to just be, how to live life to the full, and how to be at peace with everything and everyone around us. These answers lead us also to be at peace with ourselves. The strongest foundation anyone can ever have."

Thinking back to all he had witnessed by George's side and the lessons played out before him, Josh realised they were there for him to recognise, and reap the rewards.

"To live in the moment, to trust and be open," Josh spoke his thoughts aloud. "Follow your heart. Let go and believe in yourself."

"You see what happens, Josh? These answers develop within us a new way of seeing, thinking and doing. In return, they fill our lives and the deep cavities our hearts with the happiness and contentment craved for."

"But how? How will these answers come?"

George once again saw Josh burned to know more. Waiting for him to relax his pause only made Josh more agitated.

"How?"

"Josh, all the answers are already inside you. They are buried deep within everyone, lying dormant, waiting to be discovered."

"The answers to everything?"

"Yes, everything. You just have to awaken them. Sometimes the process is long and hard, but the biggest hurdle is to realise these answers lay within us all in the first place."

"But, how do I awaken these answers?"

"Slow down. Small steps, remember? These answers found within only become apparent when ready to be recognised."

"But, I want them now," Josh demanded.

Untouched by Josh's outburst, George remained calm.

"Only when you are ready. If you grab at these answers they will simply move further from you. All you will be doing is pushing them away far out of reach. All answers have a natural flow unique to everyone. Revealed to us when ready and never before."

"Well, if they're there for the taking, why wait?"

"If the answers come to us without the lessons beforehand we would discard them frivolously. Take them for granted and not for the precious jewels they are."

With those words Josh realised how he had acted.

"There you go," George said. "Another lesson learnt and answered."

"To have patience."

"So, how do you feel?"

"Bad," Josh replied.

Ashamed of his actions, he thought how George had shown nothing but kindness and respect towards him and in return he had acted like a spoilt child.

"Do not feel bad, Josh. We all slip from time to time. It is in the realisation we have done so that is the crucial part. We often learn the hard way, by our mistakes. But, once learnt never forgotten."

Josh turned to the window beside him. He listened to the train's melodic beat as it careered along its tracks, his thoughts centered on what he had learnt so far.

CHAPTER TWELVE

The subway train slowed and came to a halt before another busy station. Still feeling some guilt from his attitude earlier Josh was first to his feet and waited for George at its open doors.

George could see what played on Josh's mind.

"Ready?" He said as they stepped out onto the platform together.

Though not as hectic as their previous stop commuters still swamped the two. Josh and George battled their way to the platform's revolving green gate acting as both entrance and exit to the station. In single file they climbed a flight of stairs and out onto the street.

Cold, crisp air, took Josh by surprise. Buttoning his jacket he looked above him. Dark clouds formed as the sky descended into dusk. Turning to George he pointed to the subway sign next to them.

"We're still in the city?"

"Yes, a full eight months further on since our last stop."

A rumble from the clouds above enhanced the evening rush home of those around them.

"We had better hurry too," George said as the storm approached and led Josh away from the subway entrance.

Walking by small restaurants and convenience stores drain outlets steamed in the roadway bedside them. With vapours swirling as cars raced through them Josh recalled how he had somehow known the way to the hospital. Now this place seemed strangely familiar to him also.

A thunderclap snapped through the air and Josh felt rain spot the top of his head.

"This way." George pulled his coat collars up around his neck as they rounded a corner and into a suburban neighbourhood.

Walking between the two story homes lining the street, orange lanterns of skulls and witches decorated small balconies, each holding carved pumpkins grinning menacingly down onto passersby. The skies rumbled again, this time bringing rain with it.

"Quick," George pointed to the house beside them. "Let us wait here until the rain stops."

Following George down a small path, a porch light lit their way between neat lawns covered with orange and yellow leaves. George stopped at the porch's three wooden steps and sat down. Josh lowered himself down beside him.

Both sheltering from the heavy rain Josh looked to his feet and the irreversible stains now across his shoes. He no longer cared if they were ruined. All that mattered now was his journey, and wherever they would be going to next once the rains had stopped.

As darkness set in around them they listened to the rain's crashing rhythm, its fine drops brought to life as watery pins when caught in a passing car's headlights.

Josh looked up to a squeal of laughter.

Two figures ran hand in hand across the street and down the path to where he and George sat.

"Here they are," George said.

The young couple laughed together even though both soaked from the downpour.

Wearing the young man's worn jean jacket over hospital scrubs, the young woman's red hair poked out beneath a white knitted woolen hat. Shoulders hunched, the young man jogged beside her in jeans and T-shirt. Josh began to stand as they raced towards the porch.

"Wait a moment," George whispered.

Coming to a stop at the foot of the wooden steps the young couple turned and faced each other.

Her dark brown eyes mesmerised the young man. They shone and sparkled with life, a sparkle he knew would never leave them. Reaching over he lifted a strand of wet red hair from her cheek. Edging closer their lips met as cold raindrops streamed over them, warming faintly between where her skin joined with his.

Josh felt no discomfort so close to such an intimate moment. The way the young couple kissed seemed right, natural.

A loud mewing distracted their tender clinch.

"Namoo," the young woman called out.

Breaking away she picked up the black cat at her feet. The young man glared at their interruption.

'Shhh, you'll hurt her feelings," she kissed the cat cradled in her arms.

Josh and George moved aside as the young woman unlocked the front door.

"Wait," the young man said as she opened it.

"What?"

"This."

Holding the door open with his foot, he cupped her face in his hands and drew her close. They fell softly into each other once more. The cat scrambled from the young woman's arms. She let her escape and wrapped herself round her Noa Koo. As the cat nudged the front door open George saw his chance.

"Quick," he said.

Both he and Josh slipped past the young couple's embrace and followed the patter of wet paws up a short flight of stairs to the house's second floor apartment.

Two mountain bikes leant against the banister at the top of the stairs. Josh knocked into one of them. Catching it as it began to topple the cat looked up. Staring at Josh with piercing green eyes she purred once and returned to scratch fresh claw marks into the apartment's door as laughter echoed up the stairs.

"Get off me," the young woman giggled. The young man continued to grab playfully at the back of her calves.

"I'm warning you," she said, secretly not wanting him to stop.

Opening their home's front door the cat darted past her and the young couple followed, unbeknown to them on that wet autumnal night two uninvited guests did so also.

CHAPTER THIRTEEN

Entering the young couple's apartment, Josh and George squeezed past the young man as he closed the door after them with the back of his heel.

The young woman scampered through the apartment's small living room, into the kitchen and through another door. She re-appeared to the sound of running water.

"Catch," she called.

Josh ducked as a large towel flew across the room. Winking to the young man, she disappeared back into the bathroom as he caught it, prompting him to chase after her leaving a trail of wet clothes across the floor. As the bathroom door slammed shut behind him the cat jumped then returned to lap her fur dry.

Josh joined George on the large worn blue couch that dominated the room.

"Nice place," he said.

The mix of old and new furniture sat well with colourful artwork adorning the walls of the tiny home. A large oil painting of a Buddha in shades of brown and cream smiled down on Josh and George, accompanied by a painting of a brightly coloured Geisha, her eyes also rested on unknown guests.

"Recognise anything, Josh?"

Looking to the large orange and yellow blanket hung next to the door they had just entered Josh studied its intricate patterns of stitches, mirrors and beads.

"It all looks very Asian to me," he said.

"Yes, it is."

"Where they first met?"

"One year ago to the day," George smiled.

"Looks like they brought a piece of Asia home with them," Josh looked to the objects dotted around him.

"I suppose they did, but that is not only what they brought back with them." George gazed around the room and then focused back on Josh. "They brought back all they had learnt about themselves, all which had been awakened within them. The essence of just being with an openness allowing them to glimpse how things may work."

George nodded over to the bathroom and the laughter seeping from under its door escorted by clouds of hot steam.

"Many find the spirit of their true selves," George continued, "when far from home and in unfamiliar territory. They often become who they really are. For they have no restrictions and the freedom to explore. To discover what they are and sometimes what they are not meant to be. They get to follow their own unique path."

Josh saw a hint of sadness in George's eyes.

"But, when they return home and are back on familiar ground, the freedom they found whilst away can become stifled and ebb from their grasp. They sometimes become pulled in another direction, off their path and away from their own story."

"Story?"

"You entered into this world on your own, and one day you will leave alone. What happens inbetween is your story, no one else's, just yours. To live your life how you want it to be on your own path."

"But isn't that a selfish way to live?"

"On the contrary, it is quite the opposite. To live your life exactly how you want to live it is not selfish, not at all. But to ask or guide someone else into living a life how you think it should be lived then there, that is where selfishness lies."

George began to smile.

"Josh, no one knows the right way to be or the correct way to live. Different ways of life suit different people. But, everyone must be allowed to follow their own story, walk their own path and go their own way."

Josh looked to the bathroom and its continued giggles within.

"What about these two," he said. "Don't they have their own stories, their own paths?"

"True, they do have their own individual paths, yet they still live how they want to live. It was they who choose to be together, albeit with a little help from the hands of fate. No one else choose for them. They still had freewill to make this decision, and although they are terribly in love they are in no way co-dependent on each other. This allows for each of their separate unique paths to fit effortlessly together and to continue side by side in harmony, almost touching but not quite."

Josh could see how the young couple complemented each other. There was understanding and respect flowing between them. He also saw how they had retained the spirit of all they had discovered in their time away, both together and alone.

The cat padded across the floor to them. She jumped up and settled in George's lap.

"Namoo," George whispered to her. "The essence of what they brought back is all around us, Josh," he stroked under the cat's chin and she purred beneath his touch.

Josh looked down to the contentment on the cats face.

"Namoo," George whispered again. "Namaste."

"Namaste? What does that mean?"

"It means many things in many languages. Hello, welcome, how are you? It is also said it is the first thing said between soul mates when they find each other again."

Namoo stirred. Leaping from George's lap she made her way to a wicker basket in one corner of the room. She nestled down amongst its colourful balls of wool as the bathroom door swung open.

Unaware of their audience the young couple ran naked through the apartment. Josh and George smiled to the calls of coldness coming from the bedroom.

The young woman appeared first. In vest top and jogging shorts she waltzed through to the kitchen.

"I'm so hungry," she said opening the refrigerator door. "No way, you've got to be kidding."

"What's up," the young man slipped on jeans and T-shirt in the doorway of the bedroom. "Is that all we have?" He stared at the dishevelled onion in the young woman's hand.

"What are we going to do?" She said, hand on hip.

The young man smiled.

"I know," he said. Kicking on his shoes he dug into his pockets. "Two dollars thirty-five," he counted the loose change in his hand.

"Leave it to me," he threw on a jacket and raced out of the apartment.

The young woman shook her head and walked over to the cat.

"Namoo, Namoo, Namoo," she said, greeted by sleepy feline eyes.

"Where's he gone?" Josh said.

"Shopping."

"With a couple of dollars?"

"You have to remember they are still students. Bills come and go, and this time for them now is quite hard. But, they still manage to keep a roof over their head and…"

"And they have each other," Josh looked over to the young woman. George nodded.

"No matter how trying times can be, materially and emotionally, you always have as much as you need at that present moment."

Lighting a small gas heater next to the cat, the young woman switched on the small lamp beside Josh. Draping a red silk scarf across its shade she walked to the bedroom in the room's warm glow. She returned with two white candles and a stick of incense.

Josh and George watched her prepare the low table in front of them. With a lit candle on either end she placed a burning incense stick in its centre. Putting on some music with volume low, she pulled up a couple of cushions, leant back on the couch and looked up to the clock above the door.

The world outside rumbled again and Namoo woke with a start to a clap of thunder. Traipsing over to the young woman she snuggled down on her. Listening to rain lashed windowpanes the young woman glanced up to the clock once more.

"Where is he?" She asked the bundle of black fur in her lap.

Namoo purred softly back at her as lightening lit up the living room. Looking to the clock for a third time she watched a smoky trail of incense meander upwards to a warm red ceiling.

CHAPTER FOURTEEN

A long track of incense ash fell onto the table as the front door burst open. The young woman woke with a start.

"Where have you been?" She jumped to her feet.

"Everywhere was closed," the young man said. "I had to walk five blocks." He hung up his jacket and shook the rain from his hair. "But I got this," he held up a wet brown paper bag as he walked by Josh and George.

"What have you got there then?"

"Dinner," the young man called out from the kitchen.

Josh and George followed her smile into the apartment's small kitchen. The young man had already started to dice their lone onion. Leaning against the sink the young woman watched him.

"Let's see what we're having then," she delved into the grocery bag.

"Potato chips?" She placed the family sized bag beside her. "Cilantro, one red pepper and an orange," she giggled.

"Leave it to me," he took the items from her.

"Ok, ok," she said, her arms high in the air.

Leaving the crack and sizzle of hot oil Josh and George followed her back into the living room.

Within minutes the young man appeared from the kitchen, a full plate in each hand. He placed a dish of fried, diced onions sprinkled with red peppers and green herbs before her. Potato chips garnished their meal.

"What do you think?" The young man asked as she took a chip from her plate.

"They're hot," she said in surprise on taking a bite.

"Well yeah, I grilled them."

"You what?" She laughed. "Come here." She pulled him close and kissed him on the forehead.

"I got this too," he produced a small can of beer.

"Priorities?" She laughed again.

As they ate and took alternate sips from the beer can neither of them talked, but would look up to each other and smile.

"It actually smells and looks quite good," Josh said.

"It certainly does. Although it is not just the ingredients that makes it so appealing, Josh."

"The company?"

"That as well, but the real secret lies in the preparation. The care and attention that went into making this meal adds to its tatse."

Josh could see how much the young couple enjoyed their meagre meal.

"You see, Josh. You always have exactly as much as you need."

Finishing their meal the young woman took the plates into the kitchen. She retuned head bowed in concentration, her fingers peeling the orange's outer skin careful as not to waste a bit. Pulling up her cushion next to the young man she handed him half of their dessert.

Savouring each segment she lay down, her head rested on the young man's lap. Orange had never tasted so sweet.

In contentment she told him of her day. Listening to the stories of her new hospital placement closer to home and the incidents that took place there, the young woman told him how she could not wait for the next six months to pass when she would no longer be regarded as a student nurse.

The young man's fingertips gently combed across her eyebrows. The tones of her voice where always a comfort and often carried him through his day played soothingly in his memories. He stroked her temple and massaged its tender hollow with circles of soft pressure. Beginning to relax her body eased and any anxieties melted away. Looking up to him under sleepy eyelids her hand traced up his arm and clasped the back of his neck. She pulled him down to her.

Josh and George edged their way around the young couple and stood by the front door ready to leave. Hand in hand, the young couple stood also. Josh saw the same innocence the two had held on the porch steps earlier as the young woman led her Noa Koo to the bedroom to rediscover each other and themselves once again. The door clicked behind them.

Leaving the apartment Josh began to descend the stairs. He stopped half way and stared up at George.

"Aren't we leaving?"

"No," George said. "We are going back in."

"Shouldn't we give them some privacy?"

"Is two months long enough, Josh?"

Reaching out for the banister, Josh gripped it tight and looked down.

His intuition proved right as the world developed a familiar spin and the hallway walls swirled around him.

CHAPTER FIFTEEN

Faint laughter greeted Josh and George. In a warm wave it spread across the chilled apartment from the young couple's bedroom.

Winter morning sunlight flooded the apartment and Josh looked to windows sprinkled with snowflakes. He shivered and closed the door behind him as Namoo appeared from the bedroom. Leaving its door ajar she purred up at her new guests on her way to the kitchen. George beckoned Josh to peer into the bedroom with him.

Beneath a sea of thick white duvet the young woman lay safe in her Noa Koo's arms. She nuzzled her cheek against his chest. Reaching down he kissed the top of her head. His lips stayed there. She seemed distant, her mind elsewhere. The young man sensed something bothered her and had done so for the last few weeks.

"I'm not going in today," he whispered inches from her crown.

The young woman's eyes lost their drowsy haze.

"But isn't it an important week for you?"

"I can catch up tomorrow, and well." He paused. "You've got a day off today, and I thought that…"

"You thought what?" The young woman tore herself from his warmth and stared up at him.

"I just thought we could spend the day together, just the two of us, here in bed. No work, no nothing. Just us."

The young woman's eyebrows arched.

"Well, if you'd rather me go, I…"

"No, no," she said. "You ain't going anywhere mister. You're mine all day to do with as I please," she squeezed him tight.

"Am I now?"

"You'd better believe it," the young woman giggled.

67

Josh stumbled forwards into the bedroom door causing the young couple's laughter to stop. They looked across the room.

George nudged Josh into the bedroom as the young woman clambered to the edge of the bed and pushed the door closed. Slipping back under the duvet the young man wriggled as cold hands routed for a place on his ribs. Grabbing her wrists he rolled on top of her.

"Careful," she said.

"What?"

The young man released her and sat up.

"You just have to be careful is all," she looked away, distant once more.

Kneeling up on the bed she turned to the bedroom window. Her back to him, she stared onto the snow white world outside.

"What's wrong?" Josh said.

George gave no reply.

"What's wrong?" the young man echoed Josh's words. "Are you sick?"

The young woman hesitated.

"Not really," she told him.

Kneeling up behind her he reached over to the big blue blanket next to the bed. Wrapping it around them both she leant back into him.

"Tell me, sweetheart," he said.

The young woman grasped his arms and squeezed them tight to her.

Together they looked out onto the street. In silence they watched the neighbourhood's children playing in the snow. Letting go of his arms she turned to face him.

"I'm late," she said.

"But you haven't got work today."

The young woman stared at him. She shook her head. Confused at first, the young man's eyes widened. Inching back he placed both hands on her shoulder's the delicate curve.

"As in?"

She nodded.

Bringing her back to him under the blanket's warmth they held each other close.

"What a wonderful Christmas present," he said to her.

She looked to him, her smile faint.

"I was so worried," she said.

"Why?"

"About what you'd say."

A single tear rolled down her cheek and the young man kissed it away.

"Come here," he said softly.

Laying back down on the bed she nestled into his chest once more. The young man stared up at the ceiling as they lay there as one.

"When?" He asked.

"I've tried to work it out. Remember Halloween?"

"That night we had no food?"

"Yeah, who'd of thought an onion and a pack of potato chips could be an aphrodisiac?"

"We should try and market it," he laughed glad to have her back.

She looked to him. "I have to check though."

"You're not sure?"

"Not one hundred per cent," she saw disappointment in his eyes. "But a girl knows you know. And anyway, I am a nurse." Her smile faded. "Well I nearly was."

The young man felt her sadness, sensing thoughts of a career slipping away from her.

"And you still will be," he held her close. "And if you're not I'll…"

"You'll what?"

Regaining her smiles the young woman reached for his rib cage again before resting back on the pillows.

"We'd better get one of those kit things," he said.

"Huh?"

"To check. To make sure."

The young woman became excited at the prospect.

"So much for spending the day in bed," she said.

Walking over to the bedroom mirror behind Josh and George they moved aside and she stood between them.

"Ahh, look at the state of me," she prodded at red puffy eyes.

"You look radiant," the young man teased.

Reaching down she picked his jeans up off the floor and threw them at him.

"Come on then," she laughed. "Up and at um, up and at um."

As he jumped from the bed George nodded to the door and he and Josh left the young couple to get dressed. Joining Namoo on the living room's blue couch the cat looked up at them before returning to sleep.

"Quite the morning, Josh," George rested back into the couch's soft cushions.

"Are they…"

"Are they what, Josh?"

"Are they ready?" He glanced over to the bedroom. "They seem so young."

"Josh, for a child to enter this world a parent is never ready. There is no right or wrong time no matter how young or old the expectant mother and father are." He nodded in the young couple's direction. "Josh, how lucky can this child be?"

"Lucky? But they have so little." Josh looked round the small apartment.

"They have it all. Everything they will ever need. These Noa Koo have the greatest foundation a new soul can ever possibly have. The love and respect they hold for each other contains all the security and nurturing anyone could ever dream of."

Namoo stirred next to Josh, she purred up at him as if in agreement.

"A child born from their strength of love will never want for anything. Anything at all."

Entering the room the young man handed the young woman a jacket off the back of the door.

"But they couldn't even afford a decent meal a few months ago," Josh said. "And now there will be another mouth to feed."

"Or two."

"Two? They're having twins?"

"They will manage, and they will always have enough of everything. We always do if things are important enough to us."

Leaving the couch Namoo ran to the young woman and began clawing at her jacket's white woollen cuffs.

"No Namoo, it's too cold for you out there," she picked the cat up and placed her back on the couch beside George. "We won't be long."

"Ready?" The young man lifted two woollen hats from the door and held it open.

Josh and George left their seat and ducked beneath the young man's out stretched arm and left the apartment.

From the street Josh and George watched the young couple burst from the doors of their home.

Gasping as cold frosty air hit them the young woman left a trail of petite footprints in the virgin snows as the young man caught her up and stepped over the low hedge surrounding their garden.

"Watch," the young woman called out to him.

With both feet together she jumped over the hedge to join him. Snow creaked beneath her as she landed onto the icy footpath.

Calling out as her feet rose up before her, the young man raced forwards even though he knew there was no time to catch her.

CHAPTER SIXTEEN

George blurred past Josh as compacted ice and snow loomed up to the young woman. Raising vertical her feet landed softly on the ground as the young man slid towards her.

"Did you see that?" She said.

"Are you ok?" He placed his hand onto her stomach.

"Did you see that?"

"Yes I saw it, and you told me to be careful."

The young woman glanced to the ground then back to him.

"Sorry. I'll be more careful, I promise." She began to grin. "Now there are three of us."

"Or maybe four," the young man smiled back at her.

Alarm spread across the young woman's face. She hadn't considered that possibility.

"Don't even go there," her hand chopped through the air. "Anyway, we have to make sure I am... That we are first."

Watching the young couple walk towards the end of the street Josh turned to George. "Nice catch," he said.

"Thank you," George replied.

Josh began to follow.

"Let them go," George called out.

"Huh?" Josh swung round.

"It is our time to leave them now."

"What about the results? I want to know what happens next."

George shook his head and walked to him.

"Josh, we have been witness to something so special. We have seen Noa Koo meet and recognise each other again, and watched as they have bonded and formed." Looking over Josh's shoulder to the young couple they rounded the corner ahead. "We leave them now as they prepare to bring another soul's story into this world, their union complete."

Still wanting to see more, George's words were of little compensation to Josh.

"But we can't leave them now," he said.

"We must."

"No."

Turning on his heels Josh raced after the Noa Koo. Approaching the corner of the street he felt a hard whack strike him on the back of his head. Icy slithers slipped down the collar of his shirt as he looked back at George.

"What was that for?" Josh watched George dusting snow from his hands

Rubbing the numbness at the back of his scalp he continued his pursuit of the Noa Koo. George watched him fly around the corner out of sight and then too followed the young couple's footsteps in the snow.

Josh reached up on his toes and searched within crowded streets. He felt a hand on his shoulder.

"Josh, they have gone." George whispered to him.

Staring along the street once again to see if he could spot them Josh then rubbed the back of his head again.

"Nice shot," he said.

"I had to gain your attention somehow. Shall we?" George pointed to the subway sign ahead.

Walking between people hurrying towards them with bags laden with Christmas presents, Josh and George dodged the last minute shoppers and stopped beside the subway station's entrance.

"Where to next?" Josh asked.

George took a moment to answer.

"Josh. Our journey has come to an end," he said and walked towards the subway steps.

Jostled by passersby Josh raced after him.

"We can't stop now. What happens next? Where do we go?"

George took his foot from the top of the station's stairway.

"Josh, I do not know where your next destination will be."

"Don't you mean our destination?"

"Ours?"

"Yes ours. Where are we going next?"

"Josh, it is time for us to say part ways as well."

Josh could not believe what he was hearing.

"But, you can't leave me. What do I do?" Where I am going?"

"I do not know."

"You don't know?"

"No, I do not," George shrugged. "I go back to the platform, board the train and then, then. I simply do not know."

Lost and bewildered Josh stared at the subway sign with dread. He looked back at George.

"But you can't leave me. I want to stay with you."

George shook his head.

"Our time together is over, Josh."

"But why?"

"You have to understand that people come in and out of our lives all the time. Each one we meet we gain something from. They all have a message for us, good or bad. A meeting of minds to help us along our path."

Shock continued to course through Josh as George continued.

"When these people leave us we must let them go. Let them continue with their stories and pass on their knowledge to others, as you must pass on yours also."

George held his hand out to Josh.

"Well, it was nice meeting you," he smiled.

"Is that it? Is that all you can say?"

With no words George nodded down to his hand. Hesitant at first Josh took it to shake goodbye. George's grip tightened. As Josh tried to pull away the clasp only became stronger.

"How much, Josh? How much more do you want to see?" Strong winds picked up along the street, they roared and circled the two. "Tell me. What do you want?" George shouted over the din.

"I want to see more," Josh shouted back.

He felt George search far within him, deep inside where even he had never looked. The city streets began to strobe around them and day turned into night and back again at a frightening rate, the snow beneath their feet melting to reveal harsh grey slabs.

The winds decreased as time slowed back down and George's grip slackened into a tender hold.

He smiled to Josh under a spring sky of vivid blue.

CHAPTER SEVENTEEN

"Are you ready to continue?" George asked.

Only now did Josh realise all he had seen, felt and experienced on his journey was no longer a game or façade. George had unleashed a tremendous power. Now the rules had changed.

"Are you ready?" George asked again.

"Yes. I'm ready," Josh said.

Together they walked from the subway station steps. Leaving the young couple's home far behind they walked block after block without a word.

In a spring afternoon's warmth Josh removed his coat as they approached a convenience store. George stopped and waited for him outside its doors.

"Lovely day," George looked to the trees beside them.

"Yes," Josh joined George's view up to pink and white buds on the verge of blossom. "What happened back there?"

"Sometimes we need a little push. A slight nudge to help us leave our old ways of thinking behind."

"But that was a bit more than a nudge."

"I suppose it was," George smiled. "Sometimes we receive subtle clues in our lives to expand our ways of thinking, small hints that lead us to see the world around us in a different light." He paused and admired the trees again. "When we do not notice these clues, or see them and give no attention then we receive a jolt. Our world is shaken to awaken us to what we may be missing."

"So I was missing something?"

"We often come up against hardships and shocks in our lives Josh. Times can be difficult, but these moments all serve a purpose.

They are there to unlock what sleeps within us. To help us break free of old thoughts and move onto another higher level of understanding."

"Well you certainly jolted me. You scared me to death. That is if I'm not already."

"Well it worked, did it not?"

Josh nodded. He felt something had stirred within him and pushed him on to look at things from a different angle.

The convenience store's bell rang behind them and Josh gave a double take to who left its doors.

"Yes, it is him," George confirmed Josh's thoughts.

Dressed in a navy suit the young man stood before them, his long dark locks now replaced by a short neat haircut.

Delving into a paper bag he produced a greetings card and smiled down to the large pink heart spread across its cover. Slipping it into his jacket pocket he looked to his watch and hurried down the street.

"Is it February?" Josh said.

"It is Valentine's Day tomorrow. Less than two months after we last left him and his Noa Koo. Let us see where he is going," George said, a remoteness in his voice. "You said you wanted to see more."

Following the young man onto a short street he led them down the pathway of a large house. Josh and George slid behind him through its front door. Climbing the house's three flights of stairs they entered through a large oak door at its summit opened by the young man.

"Hey," he called, hanging his jacket on the back of the door and tucking the Valentine's card back down into his pocket out of sight.

"I'm in here," the young woman's voice replied. "What are you doing home so early?"

Josh and George followed him through the new apartment. They passed Namoo asleep on a familiar blue couch. She stirred and purred a sleepy hello to them both.

Smells of fresh paint greeted them as they continued down a hallway. The young man walked through the door at its end.

"My boss let me finish early for the weekend," he said with Josh and George following him into the small room.

Incense burned in one corner to mix sweetly with a strong odour of paint. The young man looked to the figure in front of him and then to the half-finished wall of pink. A rush of red hair swung round as the young woman looked over her shoulder to him. Under a men's white shirt smattered with pink Josh saw the gentle curve of the young woman's stomach.

"Nice job," the young man said.

His Noa Koo smiled and continued to paint. Moving in behind her he nestled his chin into her shoulder.

"Namaste," she whispered to him.

"Namaste," the young man spread his arms around her. "How are we both today?"

Turning around to kiss him, he closed his eyes. He sprung back as to the dab of pink on the end of his nose.

"Right." The young man removed his tie.

Pretending to avoid him with playful denials, she soon succumbed to his advances and they kissed.

Returning to the wall the young woman spread a large vertical strip of pink as far as she could reach. The young man watched her shirt rise to reveal her thighs. Looking over her shoulder she caught his gaze.

"Hey, that thing's not going to build itself," she pointed across the room with the end of her paintbrush. A half assembled crib lay beneath the window "And that look of yours, mister." she added. "Is what got us into this situation in the first place."

The young woman returned to her painting and smiled into a wall of pink.

Picking up a screwdriver the young man set to work and Josh watched on as they prepared for their new arrival.

"You still haven't told me how you know it's going to be a girl," the young man said from under the crib.

"I just know," the young woman edged closer to the walls. "You come up with any more names yet?"

The young man grinned. She knew what was on his mind.

"No," she said. "We're not naming her after every player for the New York Yankees."

He laughed as she walked over to him.

"This little girl ain't going to be no baseball player," she patted her small bump. Rising up onto his knees he placed a hand on either side of her hips and gave her stomach a kiss.

"This little one will be whatever she wants to be," he said as the young woman tousled his hair and smiled down at him. "She will never want for anything," he kissed the same spot again. Lost for a moment within each other they finally broke free.

"Come on, we've got work to do," she said. Stepping back she admired her handy work then left the room. She soon returned.

"No." the young man saw the chair she had carried from the kitchen.

"Why not? I haven't finished yet," she pointed up to the horizontal strip of white where wall met with ceiling.

"I'll do that bit in a minute," he said.

"But it's not that high," she protested.

"No," the young man glared at the chair again.

Placing the chair down next to George the young woman leant on the window ledge behind the young man. Smiling again at her pink masterpiece she then looked down to him. She nudged his elbow with her toes as he tried to fix a screw into their new one's crib. He ignored her for as long as he could before frowning up at her.

"What?" She said innocently.

"Josh," George whispered and gestured to the door. Leaving the soon to be nursery they joined Namoo on the couch.

Josh stretched out next to the cat and looked around the young couple's new apartment. The same large orange and yellow blanket hung next to the front door and paintings of Buddha and Geisha continued to smile down on them from the walls.

"So they moved." He said.

"When they found out of their new arrival the young man finished college and found work in the city as an apprentice architect, and the young woman still works as a nurse."

Josh sensed something bothered George. His newfound respect for his friend stopped him from prying. He knew George would tell him when, and if he was ready.

The young man left the nursery and walked past them.

"They seem so happy," Josh watched him whistle his way to the kitchen.

"Yes, Josh, they do," George whispered back.

He closed his eyes as the young man returned with two cups of steaming coffee. They remained closed as a loud crash and scream came from the end of the hallway.

The cups fell from the young man's grasp and Josh sprinted after him as shards of porcelain shattered across dark wooden floorboards.

CHAPTER EIGHTEEN

The young man jumped to his feet and barged past George to the hallway phone.

George walked to the young woman and knelt down beside her. Placing a hand on her cheek he whispered to her. The young woman's eyelids fluttered open, her confused stare replaced by newfound innocence beneath George's words. She smiled up to him and nodded in understanding.

Removing his hand her eyes closed once more and he returned to Josh's side. The young man raced back into the room. As he began to stroke her eyebrows the young woman's eyes opened to his touch.

"I'm sorry," she said to him.

"It's nobody's fault, I'm here now," he combed his fingers across her brow.

Shock wound its way through the young man. Knowing he had to be strong for her now he hid his fear as best he could. Reaching forwards his lips lingered on her forehead. The young woman smiled over to George and her hand lifted up to give him a faint wave. George smiled to her and her hand dropped to the floor as her eyes closed once more.

"They won't be long," the young man said to her. "They won't be long," he repeated for his own reassurance.

Fighting back tears he continued to stroke her brow. Josh turned to the loud rap sounding behind him and moved aside as the young man vaulted past him to the front door.

"In here," he led the two paramedics towards his Noa Koo.

They hurried after him asking a barrage of questions.

"What's happened here?" The one paramedic knelt down.

Her kind tones unlocked the young woman's sleep.

"Can you tell me your name?"

The young woman could only mumble back to her.

"It's ok, you're going to be just fine."

The paramedic took her partner aside. Their hushed conversation lasted seconds.

Watching on helplessly as the paramedics hoisted the young woman onto a stretcher, the young man dashed down the hallway, grabbed his jacket and held the front door open for them as his love drifted in and out of reality. Josh and George also followed down three flights of stairs and climbed into the awaiting ambulance outside.

"Ok," the paramedic shouted to her colleague from the driver's cabin, the young woman safely strapped in.

Swaying from side to side in early evening traffic Josh and George grabbed hold of the ambulance's door handles. They watched the paramedic pierce the young woman's arm with the sharp end of an IV's tail. Reaching to hang its bag of saline on the hook above the young woman she instead handed it to the young man.

"Here, hold this. High," she instructed out of kindness to aid the young man's helplessness.

The paramedic checked the young woman again. Josh saw her worried looks and then noticed the blanket covering the young woman. Deep red had begun to bleed through its white fabric below her midriff. The paramedic rushed to the front of the ambulance.

"We're losing her," she mouthed to the driver over the ambulance's shrill siren.

The young man stared down at the blanket.

"What's wrong? What's happening?" He demanded. The paramedic returned to his side.

"Talk to her," she said taking the IV from him. "Speak to her, she needs you now."

The young man leant close to his Noa Koo's cheek and began to recount the story of how they first met.

Describing the lake and the restaurant where she had first passed by only to return, his voice wavered recalling the rooftop that same evening. He told her of the clear night sky and of the pink snow-capped mountains that had greeted them in the morning. The young woman murmured as he spoke of their first kiss.

"You can't leave me yet, we've only just found each other again," he said, her hand held tight in his.

The ambulance came to a sharp halt and its doors swung open. Josh and George leapt from them and made way for the hospital's welcoming committee of doctors and nurses. They listened as the paramedics brought them up to speed then wheeled the young woman through to the emergency room. The young man fought for place amongst them.

"You have to leave her with us," a nurse told him as they approached a set of doors. The young man looked at her in despair and barged past her. A doctor looked up.

"Get him out of here," he shouted.

Ignoring him, the young man ran to the young woman only for a security guard to pull him back.

"Get off me," he yelled. The clench around him to grew stronger.

George left Josh's side and went to the two men. He placed a hand on their shoulders. The security guard released his hold and the young man fell silent as he watched his love disappear from sight, staring at the growing patch of burgundy across her abdomen. He turned to hurried footsteps behind him.

"Diane," he called.

The young nurse took him in her arms. He fell into her.

Josh and George followed them into an empty waiting room and sat down opposite the young man and the young nurse.

"She's in good hands," she said.

"I only left her for a minute," he said. "How could I have been so stupid?"

"Hey," Dianne told him.

The young man focused on her.

"It's no one's fault. I'm going to be with her. Don't worry, we both know she's a fighter," she smiled, her feistiness legendary to them both.

"Wait here." Diane kissed him on the top of his head and ran from the waiting room.

Watching her leave the young man leant forwards. With his elbows on his knees Josh mirrored his posture as George walked over to the young man and sat beside him.

The young man subconsciously folded into George and succumbed to his embrace. Stillness filled the room as the three of them sat silent in an air of calm.

George returned to sit beside Josh as a young doctor walked into the room. Josh noticed a smear of blood on the lapel of his white coat.

Recognising him from his Noa Koo's old hospital, the sight of a familiar face gave the young man some renewed hope. The doctor walked to him head bowed trying to avoid the optimistic stares awaiting him.

George pointed to the entrance of the waiting room and he and Josh left their seats to listen to the doctor from its doorway. His words transformed the young man's expectant expression from fear, to disbelief, and then sorrow.

Josh's wet cheeks glistened from the doctor's sad news.

"They were looking forward to her arrival so much. They prepared everything ready," Josh said. He wiped his eyes as George turned to him. "How could this happen to them? How can a child's life be taken away so early? Before it's even begun?"

Josh looked to the heartbroken young man staring down at the floor. Diane rushed back into the room.

"It is time for us to go," George said and walked away.

Josh wasn't ready to leave and hovered in the doorway.

"You can go see her now," Diane said as the young man continued to stare at the floor.

"She's going to be ok, she's asking for you. She needs you."

Tears ran from the young nurse as the young man reached into his jacket pocket.

They both looked down to the Valentine's card in his hands, and as the young man gently rubbed his thumb over its pink heart he began to cry.

CHAPTER NINETEEN

Josh felt little comfort returning to the confines of the subway car. In search of distraction he stretched out in his seat arms folded and stared to the ceiling.

"What will happen to them?" He said. "What will they do now?"

"They will get through this," George said.

"But how?"

"Through this tragedy their bonds will be complete. Nothing can separate them now. They will find the strength within themselves to move on from this."

"How will they cope? How can they pull through this?" Recalling the deep sorrow that had filled the waiting room he turned to the window beside him and stared out into the tunnel's dark shadows.

"They will both get through these challenging times," George reassured. "The love they contain for each other surpasses all else. It holds a special, unique quality. It is purely unconditional. There is no need to worry for them. For they mourn not for themselves, but for each other. They are more concerned of the others sorrow than that of their own."

Thinking of the love that flowed between the young couple Josh remembered their reunion at the train station and how they met once again in the hospital hours later. Recalling the young couple's meagre dinner in their first home on a wet autumnal night, Josh saw how the young couple had put the needs of the other before their own without hesitation. He knew they would always be there for one another. Selflessness had shone from them throughout their journey, a journey Josh now felt such a part of.

Understanding how the young couple would both overcome this

tragedy together his fears for them began to drift away.

The train lurched forwards and began to accelerate.

Josh held onto his seat as the subway car careered down its tracks at an impossible speed.

"What, happening?"

"We are going onwards," George said. "There is still more to see."

As the subway car rattled and whined around him, Josh looked to the lights flashing throughout the carriage. Moments later the constant push into the back of his seat eased and the train began to slow. On coming to a smooth halt the carriage doors slid open without a sound onto a deserted platform.

"Shhh," George raised a finger to his lips.

A slight breeze whipped past them as they walked across the empty platform and entered a dark corridor. A doorway's dim light lay at its end.

In the darkness Josh's foot found a discarded beer can. Its metallic echo rang across unseen tiled walls. George raised a finger to his lips again as the corridor filled with warm sunlight and a shrill cry flowed from the doorway before them. It was soon joined by another's tiny wail.

A blurred figure rushed across the doorway entrance and George hurried forwards into the room ahead. By the time Josh entered also George was gone, leaving him bathed in rays of summer sunlight blanketing a well-furnished living room.

The room filled with more cries and Josh turned to their source. With a smile George beckoned to him from the end of a short hallway to the room of cries. On joining him, Josh looked through the doorway to what had given such joy.

Beneath a hanging mobile of coloured shapes a double crib lay between walls of baby blue. Cradled in a wooden cocoon two small pink faces peeked out from under a soft blue blanket.

The young woman reached into the crib to subdue her children's calls. One twin stopped crying and gave her a newly mastered smile before nuzzling into his brother's cheek to comfort him until he too fell silent.

"That's better guys," the young woman said to them.

Both looked up to their mother. Mesmerised by her swing of red hair tiny eyelids soon closed to become lost in dreams of colours and shapes they had only just begun to glimpse.

"Keep an eye on my boys, Namoo," the young woman instructed. The cat purred under her soft touch and with a brief glance to Josh and George returned to watch over her family's new additions.

Leaving the nursery the young woman turned to the crib and its blue bundle rising and falling to her boy's small breaths.

A phone's ringing broke her tranquil spell. She looked to the timepiece on her nurse scrubs with unease and dashed to the living room to answer its constant rings. The young woman raised the receiver to her ear.

"Hello, oh hey," she smiled. "Yeah good, you? They're fine. Where are you? You should have been here twenty minutes ago."

The young woman's eyes beginning to glisten.

"You're what? But, you knew I was working today. Can't you get out of it? They work you enough there as it is."

Her face flushed red.

"No, I can't ask her again. Diane covered for me last week, when you had to work late. Again," she added. "You promised. You know how important my work is to me, you're not the only one with a career you know. I only have three shifts a week. Just three."

Her jaw clenched to the phones answer.

"No I can't, you know how hard it is to get a sitter these days. Anyway, where am I going to find one in five minutes?"

The young woman looked up to the shelves in front of her. A happy couple smiled back from a silver photo frame, frozen in moments of joy. With a much different expression the young woman's view fleeted over the two snug rings on her left hand.

"Fine, fine. Just remember they're your kids too."

The phone slammed down into its cradle.

Slumping down on the arm of the couch she looked to her watch and then her work clothes. A new set of tears filled the home as fresh cries erupted from the nursery.

"Stay here," George whispered to Josh.

He raced towards the boys.

The young woman headed for them too. She stopped as wails changed into tiny giggles before fading into silence. George reappeared beside Josh as the young woman reached for the phone and began to dial.

"Diane? Hey. Yeah fine. Well…"

Her voice quivered.

"Oh, it's nothing really," she sniffed. "Just me being silly is all." She looked to the wedding photo again. "Can I ask a favour?" She cringed. "Can you cover for me again, please? Today?"

Josh felt tension rise in the room as the young woman waited for an answer.

"Yes, he's working late, again. I've got no one to look after the boys and, and…Oh thank you Diane. I'll never ask again, I promise."

The young woman fought back her tears.

"I know, I know, but he's doing so well at the company and…"

Her sobs burst forward. Listening to her friend she sat up straight.

"No," she wiped her cheeks. "No Diane, that hadn't even crossed my mind."

Continuing to listen she glanced to the summers evening outside.

"No, he wouldn't, he couldn't. He's just been busy… No Diane, I won't do that. I trust him, I trust him with all my heart." She paused. "No, I couldn't follow him. That would be betraying all we have together, I just couldn't do it."

The young woman looked out of the window once more.

"He's just been busy, that's all. Although… Oh it's nothing really. Well, lately, when we've put the twins to bed and finally got some time for us, one moment he's here, then it's like he's drifted off to another place. Somewhere else, distant."

The young woman remained silent, and then smiled.

"Anyway, I've got the boys, I could hardly take them with me, could I? No, I know you love looking after them. It's not going to happen Diane. Like I said, I trust him."

The young woman looked up as sleepy stirrings came from the nursery once again.

"Look, I've got to go. Thanks Diane, I owe you one." She began to laugh. "Don't worry I'll make it up to you, I promise. You take care too, bye."

Relieved although holding some guilt Diane had agreed to cover for her, the young woman walked to the nursery. Josh and George followed behind her.

Stopping at the hallway mirror she sighed at the red eyes staring back at her then went to her boys.

"Daddy's gone and done it again boys," she whispered into the crib. "It's just you guys and me tonight."

Another tear fell from the young woman.

"What's wrong?" Josh said.

"They have been planted," George replied. "It is time for us to go."

"Where are we going now?" Josh said.

"Tomorrow."

"Tomorrow? But wait, what happened back there? What's been planted?"

George turned to Josh.

"The seeds of doubt," he said as the world began to spin around them.

CHAPTER TWENTY

Tall buildings climbed up to meet bright blue summer skies, the narrow streets below lost in shadow. Josh steadied himself and stared upwards over walls of steel and glass.

"Impressed, Josh?" George asked.

With a nod Josh looked out into the crowded street before them. Business people scurried past, jackets slung over their shoulders in the city's lunchtime heat.

"Josh," George called.

Josh stumbled sideways before he could answer.

"Sorry," a businessman shouted back. He raised his hand without a glance to who he had walked into and marched ahead.

"Always the next thing," George said.

"What next thing?" Josh watched the businessman become engulfed in the crowds.

"So many strive for the next thing that will make them happy. And when that next purchase arrives? The happiness they expected simply is not there, and so they set another goal to reach that elusive happiness."

"And when they reach their new target, they're still not happy?"

"They cannot see the happiness they strive so much for rests within them. All they have to do is stop for a moment and see it is already there, and has been all along without these pursuits of fool's gold." He turned to Josh. "What do you think will be going through their mind in the closing moments of their lifetime? Do you think they will fondly recall the business deals they made valued so much and wish they had spent more time in the office? Will they remember the numbers and figures that became the surrogate family they said they would have when their bank balance reached a certain height, but never found time for?"

Staring into the masses, Josh saw futures of lost moments and regrets never to be recouped.

"Sorry," a voice called out.

Josh ricocheted from another blow and another arm raised to reaffirm an apology.

"Hey," Josh shouted. "What's your probl…"

"Yes," George saw Josh recognised his assailant. "We have been waiting for him."

They followed young man's confident stride through human traffic until he reached the end of the street and turned its corner.

Josh stopped. The place seemed familiar to him on catching sight of a bronze bull statue lunging to its side. George saw this and beckoned Josh to continue their pursuit of the young man. Together they rounded the corner after him.

Suits and haste gave way for less hurried pedestrians. The young man had stopped in front of small store. Its entrance draped with flowers he looked up to its sign and walked into the florists.

"We can see from here," George pointed to the flower shop's window.

Peering under half open blinds shielding blooms from harsh midday sun, a man in a green apron welcomed his new client from behind a dark oak counter.

Ushering the young man from one flower stand to another the florist would pause, tenderly lift the head of a flower and then invite the young man to smell hidden delights. This ritual continued until the young man's solitary choices developed into a bouquet of vivid colour.

"Who are they for?" Josh asked.

George gave no reply as the young man wrote a message on a small card, placed it an envelope and wrote a single capital letter on its front. He handed it to the florist who placed it on the edge of the counter.

"Can you remember, Josh?" George asked.

"Remember what? The flowers?"

"No," George smiled. "Not the flowers."

"A little. My memory, it's coming back isn't it? I remember a little. I'm sure I've walked here many times before."

He pointed across the street.

"There where I go for lunch sometimes," his finger trailed from the Thai restaurant to the small Italian coffee shop beside it. "And there, they've got great coffee."

His joy dimmed on looking to the people passing by.

"But, that's all. The faces I see are just a blur. I think I recognise someone, just for a moment, then they fade away."

"You are nearly there, Josh," George told him.

The florist door clicked open behind them. With his back to Josh and George the young man looked to his watch. He raced across the street and entered the coffee shop opposite.

"Was that all we came to see?" Josh asked.

George shook his head and motioned to a solitary figure standing a few stores from them. Looking from the florists to the coffee shop then back again, her delicate features portrayed disbelief as she brushed away strands of red hair to reveal tear filled eyes.

CHAPTER TWENTY-ONE

Josh and George shuffled aside as the young woman marched towards the flower store her husband had just left. The door handle in her grasp she gave it a sharp twist. Josh and George hurried after her until they too stood amid climbing vines and flower stands.

"Hello," the man in the green apron greeted the young woman. Ruffled by her dramatic entrance he managed to raise a smile for his new client.

"Hi," the young woman said, hiding her emotions raging within as the florist leant across the counter.

"Lovely day," he glanced outside.

The young woman followed his gaze and focused on the coffee shop opposite.

"Mmm," she looked around the surrounding assortment of flowers. Their beauty only fuelled her sadness.

"And how can I help you today?" The florist asked.

"The guy who came in here before."

The florist leant closer, intrigued by her opening words.

"Well, that guy…"

"Oh yes, I know, charming young man. Wonderful taste too. You know him?"

"Yes, I know him. At least I thought I did," she muttered. "What did he buy?"

The man came to life given the chance to talk of his passions.

"Well, first we started with carnations, red of course." He paused, "And then we added Thai jasmine followed by…" He stopped his description short. His eyes narrowed. "Why do you ask?"

"I, uh," the young woman stuttered. "Look, I just want to know who the flowers were for."

The florist recoiled.

"I can't tell you that. No, no, no," he shook his head and straightened.

"Why not?"

"Ever heard of client confidentiality?"

The young woman stared back at him.

"Yes," she snapped. "I work in a hospital. I know all about confidentiality."

"Then you will understand my position then," the florist folded his arms in defence.

Staring up to the ceiling the young woman bit into her lip. Taking a moment she returned to the florist and gave a sweet smile.

"I'm sorry. I've had a busy morning. I just want to know who the flowers were for." Her chin lowered and she looked up at him coyly.

Josh held his breath hoping the florist would melt under her charm. His hope was soon dashed.

"No, I'm sorry but I really can't help you."

"But why? Why not?" Tears welled in the young woman's eyes.

"Because, I cannot betray my customers."

The young woman's tears stopped. Her brown eyes bore into his.

"Betraying your customers? What's wrong with you? They're only flowers."

The florist gasped. "Flowers? Only flowers?" His green apron rose and fell over deep breaths.

"Please," the young woman pleaded. "Just a name, an address, anything."

The man shook his head once more and looked down to the counter. His head shot back up realising what his eyes had betrayed. He knew he was too late. The young woman had followed his stare to the small envelope below him, a capital S in blue ink across its cover. Both of them looked to each other then back to the counter.

Every muscle in the young woman's body tensed as the florist raised an eyebrow inviting her to just try.

She dived forward. At the same time the florist swept his hand down across the counter to her target. The young woman flew back and searched her hands then looked to the florist. He smiled at her from behind the counter, tapping the envelope on his bottom lip.

The young woman's stare pierced through his triumph. Holding him in her sights for a few moments she then raced towards the door and flew out into the street. Josh and George chased after her.

"You're welcome," the florist called after her.

As unaware of his farewell as she was of the traffic around her, the young woman walked through the sounds of honking horns and screeching brakes in her defiant march across the street.

Stopping outside the coffee shop she stared at its narrow door and elaborate design of Tiffany glass. Josh followed her view through the window beside her.

Sat alone in a booth of burgundy upholstered leather the young man took sips from a white cup.

The young woman shoved the ornate doors open that would lead her to her husband and Josh raced after her. He flew back into the street from the force of the swinging doors.

"Patience, Josh," George said, and entered the coffee shop first.

Striding forward the young woman faced her husband, her hand clasped on the back of the empty seat in front of him. Startled, the young man smiled up to her.

"Hello," he said.

She glared down at him.

"What's happened?" His smile left him. "What's wrong?"

His wife remained silent.

"The kids? Are they ok?"

"They're fine," she sat down opposite him. "Diane's got them."

"Oh. So, this is a nice surprise. What's up?"

The young woman still reeled from her encounter with the florist.

"I thought you could tell me that," she said and turned to the nervous waitress beside her. "Coffee please, large," she conjured up a smile from nowhere. "Black," she added before turning back to the young man. "Well?"

"Well what? Who's upset you?"

Her face flushed crimson as the young man reached over the table to her. She placed her hands in her lap.

"Oh dear," George said. "I think we should sit down, Josh."

Taking the empty booth behind the young couple, Josh shuffled along rich leather seats until he felt warm sunlight flow onto him. George lowered himself down beside him.

"But we can't see from here," Josh complained, their backs now to them.

George nodded to a framed photograph of a Venetian evening hung on the wall before them. Reflected across its glass between Gondolas on the Grand Canal under a bright Italian sky, Josh could clearly see the back of the young man's head, and the terse stares of his wife sat opposite him.

The waitress returned and placed a large cup onto their table. The young woman raised a smile and then the cup to her lips. Sipping her coffee her eyes didn't leave the young man's for an instant.

Josh and George watched as the Noa Koo remained silent, but for the clink of cups around them.

With clenched jaw the young woman eyed the customers around her. All were wrapped up in their own melodramas of laughter and chat. The young man studied her uncharacteristic mood from the other side of the table. He had only seen her this way twice before and had always put it down to her red haired temperament. He was always thankful such a temper had never been directed at him, unlike the first time. This time.

The young woman turned back to him.

"What are you doing here?" She asked.

"I'm on my lunch break. Why?"

He reached for his cup. Its contents drained, he ordered another.

"Why?" He asked again.

The young woman began to speak. She stopped as the waitress brought another coffee. Watching her hurry back to her station, she saw the waitress' workmate grin on her approach, a boyish grin the young woman knew only too well.

"So," the young woman began. "Who are the flowers for?"

"Flowers? What flowers?"

She leant over the table to him.

"Don't you give me what flowers all innocently. You know exactly what I mean." Sitting back arms folded, her eyes stayed on the young man's again.

"You followed me?" He said.

Josh and George watched the reflection of the young woman bow her head. Her sensitivity and hurt unmasked by confrontation.

CHAPTER TWENTY-TWO

"What's happened to these two?" Josh said. "You said nothing could separate them."

"Yes I did. Nothing can, but for one thing." George nodded up to the young couple's reflection. "Themselves."

"But."

"Remember, Josh, they both have their own paths, their own separate stories. They choose to be with each other, to share their lives together as one. They also choose to bring new life into this world. To nurture new souls as well as one another."

Remembering back to the joy spilling from under a bathroom door in the young couple's earlier years, Josh saw how their stories had run side by side in harmony with the others, close yet never touching. Now all he could see was the beginnings of a deep chasm between them both.

"But, Noa Koo? Kismet? Serendipity?" Josh scrambled for answers. "You said these things would not let them be."

"All the ingredients were there from the very start, right time, right place. And yes, other forces would not let them be and pushed them together time and time again."

George shifted in his seat and turned to Josh.

"You have to understand they too have a role to play in all this. They have to put the effort in, the work that will make each other's paths continue to run smoothly with the other's. Compromise, sacrifice and communication. All these things and more aid their paths to continue together side by side. It is still all up to them, Josh. They have to want this. Want this more than anything in the world." He began to smile. "Josh, they are Noa Koo, soul mates. It will not seem like work to them. It never does when you love the thing you are doing. They can walk away from this at any time, any time at all. For it is still their choice, still their own individual story and no one else's."

Looking back to them, Josh thought on George's words. Seeing how fragile the young couple's situation was Josh wanted to help them, yet he knew that even if he could it was not his place to do so. It was their story and theirs alone.

"Do not look so worried," George raised his chin back to the Venetian scene above them. "The show is not over yet."

The young man's looks of disbelief at having been followed lifted. Concern for the upset now containing his wife took its place. His hand reached out for hers.

"Hey, sweetheart," he said. "This isn't like you."

Glancing to his outstretched hand awaiting hers, she ignored his advances.

"Look. About the flowers."

"I don't care about the flowers," she raised her head. "It's you I'm worried about."

Caught in the sunlight streaming through the coffee shop window, his wife's pained expression only deepened the young man's concern.

"Where are you?" She asked him. "Where have you gone?"

The young man reached out to her once more. His hand pulled back, rejected again.

"I'm here," he said. "I'm right here with you. Every second of the day."

The young woman wiped her eyes.

"That's the thing," she turned to the window and its busy street scene beyond. "You're not," she said into its glass.

Sitting back he looked to her profile. His eyes flowed from the tiny scar above her eyebrow, the physical memory of a childhood accident, and trailed across fine cheekbones to a slight pout of lip. Features he knew so well, as familiar to him as if they were his own. He smiled as she returned from the window.

"Where have you gone?" She appealed. "Tell me. Where?"

Her words touched a place deep inside him. A place he knew only she could ever reach. Struck by her perceptiveness, the young man's soul released and his emotions lay innocent and naked before her.

"I don't know," he said. Looking out onto the street he soon returned to her.

The young woman followed the faint tears rolling from him. This time it was her hand that reached for his. With hesitation the young man moved towards her grasp. The hold he longed for when they were apart proved too poignant and his hand fell into his lap. He looked to eyes pleading for answers.

"It's just…"

"Go on, tell me," she urged.

The young man shook his head.

"No," her voice rose. "You can't stop now. Tell me, I need to know."

His attention snapped back to her.

"Let it all out," the young woman smiled. "I think you need to tell me. For yourself if nothing else."

Her smile and kind words dissolved away any final barriers surrounding him. With a freedom never experienced before the young man began to speak.

"Do you know what I look forward to all day? What I crave for when I'm not with you?" He looked into dark brown eyes willing him to continue. "All day long all I can think about is the evening when I step onto the footpath to our home. I imagine myself there, the front door facing me. I turn the key and walk in and…"

The young woman rested back, her coffee cup nestled in her hands willing him to continue.

"And then I see you. I see the kids and hear them laugh, laugh like their mother. I see myself there as I walk over to the three of you." A tear fell from him. "I look forward to that moment so much." The young man lowered his head. "So much," he said into his lap.

The young woman waited for the inevitable but. It soon came.

"But when that time actually arrives, what I thought about all day, when I finally get to see you, the twins, our home. It's just that…"

The young man stopped and looked back into his lap.

"Go on tell me," the young woman coaxed her husband to look to her.

"It's just so overpowering. I love it, I really do, all of it. Those feeling that greet me when I walk through the door is all I've ever dreamed of, and more. I long to be held in its warmth. Most of the time I let myself. It's just…"

He stared out onto the street then back to his love.

"Sometimes I get so scared of losing it all. Of losing you and the twins, the house, all of it. It's then that I can't help pushing it all away before it…"

"Before it can leave you?" The young woman nodded.

"Yes. Before it can leave me."

Surprised by her words, he began to realise this was what he had been doing all along. The young woman leant to him.

"It's all there. Me, the boys, our home. We have it all. We have each other," she said. "We've always had all we've ever needed."

"I know," the young man wiped his eyes. "I know I'm doing it, pushing it all away, and it rips me apart." His hand reached out. This time she received it and wrapped it in both of hers.

"It's always been there just waiting for you," she told him. "It's all yours, it's all ours. You just have to let it in. Let us all in." Her voice became as strong as her grip. "You are allowed this, you really are. All of it."

Pushing deep inside him once more her words symbolised all he had ever held close to him. New emotions welled within the young man. Circling and swirling through him they combined into new seeds of understanding as he stared to his hand safely cocooned inside hers.

"I'm here," she squeezed his fingers tight. "I love you."

Her hands still around his, the young woman stood and her husband shuffled along his seat as she sat down next to him. "You're my best friend," she said.

"And you're mine."

They looked to one another the way they had on the rooftop of one early Asian morning so many years ago from them now. The way they had always done throughout the years since the day they had chosen to share their lives together.

"I want it," the young man said. "I want it all."

Letting go of her hand his fingers trailed a familiar path from her eyebrow to cheekbone.

"We'll work it out," she said to him.

Stopping his gentle caress he stared at her.

"What's wrong?" The young woman reached for his hand once more. "It will be ok, it will."

"I know," he said. "I just thought I had…"

"You thought you'd what?"

"I thought I had messed everything up. I thought..."

The young woman shook her head and looked to him.

"Well you thought wrong then, didn't you. Come here," she giggled through her tears.

Falling into each other they embraced. Cloaked in fresh awareness and understanding they became lost to the world surrounding them.

In the booth behind them George turned to Josh.

"You see, Josh, they just had to want it. They had to want to be together more than anything else."

Josh nodded. "But what about the flowers?"

George encouraged Josh to look up to the young couple's reflection as a cell phone gave a muffled ring from the young woman's purse.

"Leave it," the young man said into her shoulder.

"I can't, it might be, Diane."

Looking to the concern running across her husband's face at the mention of her best friend's name she delved for her phone. Diane's number flashed across its display. The young woman sat up and grasped his hand.

"Hello, Diane, is everything ok? Ahh, good."

She leant back to the young man.

"They're fine," she mouthed to him.

"What? What does it say?" She glared at her husband. "Ok Diane, I won't be long, bye." The young woman's face reddened as her phone returned to her purse.

"What?"

"You, that's what. Why didn't you tell me?"

"Tell you what?"

"That the flowers were for me."

"They were quick," the young man glanced back to the florists. "I just remembered how much you love Thai jasmine," he said and stroked her cheek again, his voice as touch as soft as his touch. Shaking her head she leant forwards and kissed him.

At the far end of the coffee shop the young waitress wiped away a tear with her one hand and placed the other in her co-workers. He looked to her in surprise and delight. Turning to him, she lifted up onto her toes and kissed him on the cheek, reassuring her feelings matched his before returning to watch the young couple.

The young woman eased away from her husband and stood.

"Come on," she whispered to him.

"But, I've got to go back to work."

"Not today you're not, mister," she pulled him to her. "You're coming home with me," her eyes narrowed. "To do with as I please."

Embracing, the young woman's chin nestled into his chest and Josh began to stand behind them.

"No, Josh," George said. "This is their time now, our journey with them has finally come to a close."

Josh knew George was right and felt ready to leave them now. Sitting back down he watched the Noa Koo in each other's arms. The young couple began to fade out of sight, as did the coffee shop around them.

Josh felt his body lower as the soft leather seat beneath him gave way to hard plastic seats. With the subway car surrounding him and George once more any evidence of the young couple disappeared.

Glancing around the carriage he looked to George sat beside him beneath the train's familiar hum. Something was different. It took Josh a few moments to realise what that difference was.

The rows of yellow and orange seats throughout the subway car now all faced the same way towards the end of the train.

CHAPTER TWENTY-THREE

Josh spoke first in the silence he and George had held since their return to the subway car.

"I will miss them," he said.

"They are still on their journey," George eased back into his seat. "We left them the moment their paths realigned and so to run in synchronicity with the other's once more."

The warmth of the young couple's reconciliation in the coffee shop had stayed with Josh.

"So, they're going to be ok then?" He asked.

"For now," George continued to look to the end of the train.

Any peace of mind gained faded from Josh. He wanted to know more. The young couple had become such a part of him. Deep within it felt he had always known them. Although he couldn't understand why it was if he had always been with them.

"What will happen to them now? I need to know. I don't know why, I just do."

"Josh, who knows what will happen? Who knows how long things will last? Situations change, people change all the time."

Josh's anxiety grew for the young couple as George continued.

"They followed their hearts. From the first moment they met and through the years spent living together as one. As they continue to do so they still follow their dreams and hopes of a lifetime together. But, they must want it. They must want to be together. They must want to keep those separate stories of theirs from straying."

"So if they work at keeping their paths together? Then they will be ok? I mean, the young man has to let her in, let everything in…"

A familiarity struck Josh in his words. One he could almost touch yet struggled to perceive. Looking to the window beside his reflection stared back as new concepts and recognitions raced through him.

"He was scared of losing it all," Josh whispered to his mirror image. "He pushed it all away before…" He turned to George. "Before it could push him away."

"Yes, before it could push him away," George smiled. "Now he has to learn to let it all in. It may take many years for him to break this pattern as it is somewhere he finds great solace in. Familiar territory which has become a comforting place for him to return to time and time again. We all do it to a certain extent and maybe at some point so shall she. But, with the unconditional love they hold for each other they will make it work. For these are Noa Koo, Josh. The idea of a lifetime spent apart from each other is simply unimaginable."

Josh returned to his reflection.

"Let it all in," he whispered.

"They will get there. But you knew that already, did you not?"

Within George's words, Josh glimpsed why the young man's actions, mannerisms and challenges seemed so familiar to him.

Stretching back in the subway car's hard plastic seats he tried to find comfort in the train's rhythmic sway. None came to him as they hurtled further away from their previous stop and on to the next.

"How do I know?" He asked.

"You know," George looked around the subway car. "Notice anything different?"

Over chrome rails and advertising lining his metal enclosure, Josh's view fell onto rows of yellow and orange seating.

"The seats," he said. "They're all facing the same way."

"And why do think that is?"

"Are we on a different train?" Josh looked around him.

"No, same subway car."

"Then why are the seats…" Another question crept up on him. "Where are we headed to now? There is another stop, isn't there?"

George stared ahead as he spoke.

"It is time to leave all this, Josh. It is also time for our journey together to come to an end."

Apprehension rushed back to haunt Josh.

"So what happens now? Where do we…" He stopped and corrected himself. "Where do I go now?"

"That my friend," George replied. "Is still up to you."

Looking out onto the subway car's different seating arrangement Josh thought of his cloudy awareness of past of forgotten memories, and his ensuing goodbye to George

Focusing on the newspaper a few rows from him its pages lifted and settled as he tried to piece everything together.

"How can it all be up to me?" He said.

"It is still up to you where your next destination will be."

Josh's fear for his future engulfed him. A small nudge from George brought him back from his enclosed world.

"Look, it is here, Josh."

Josh followed George's stare across the subway car. In the tunnel's darkness a small orb of light hovered far in the distance. Growing in size and intensity it approached their speeding subway car, and although it shone with a blinding white pureness Josh felt no discomfort staring into its centre.

"Are you ready?" George asked beside him.

"Ready for what? What is it?"

As the orb entered their carriage its rays spilled forward.

"Go and see," George encouraged as the end of their carriage became submersed in light.

Josh took his first hesitant steps towards the light. Hypnotized by the glowing orb his stride increased. Longing to be held within its warm glow he stopped in the middle of the subway car. The orb came to a halt before him and he glanced back to George.

"Take a leap of faith, Josh." George's words entered his thoughts.

Overwhelmed by his want to enter its radiance Josh stepped forward. The light edged away for him. Taking another step the orb matched his advances and continued its retreat.

Trying to be held within its glow Josh ran down the rest of the aisle and came to a stop at its end. The orb had left the train yet continued to hover before him at a distance and he felt its warm traces on the window where his forehead now rested.

"Josh, come to me," George called to him.

Josh ignored his words, attempting to escape the sense of abandonment now surrounding him.

"Josh," George called again.

Leaving the orb Josh walked back down the aisle.

"Tell me," George asked on his return. "What did you see?"

CHAPTER TWENTY-FOUR

The orb continued to hover outside the subway car.

"It shone so bright," Josh said.

"Yes it did. What did you see?"

"It was so peaceful."

"Tell me what you saw," George asked again.

"I saw the orb come to me, it came through the window and lit up the train. I was so close to being inside it, but."

"But what, Josh?"

"But it wouldn't let me in."

"Anything else?" George pushed. "Did you see anything else?"

"Nothing. I saw it hover outside like it is now."

"I know that is what you saw, I saw that as well."

"Then what else was I supposed to see?"

"Sometimes we look at things straight on, yet never see at all."

George watched Josh become more agitated.

"I told you what I saw. I don't understand what you mean, where else was I supposed to look?"

"Within, Josh. You have to look within."

The train juddered around them as Josh reached within himself.

"I saw me. I saw me and the light, its warmth, its purity and hope. I saw how much I wanted to be inside it. It felt like coming home."

"And it would not let you in. Why do you think that was?"

"I don't know?"

"For that you must look deeper inside yourself for an answer."

Knowing the answer lay waiting patiently to be discovered, Josh's answer slowly dawned on him.

"Because I wouldn't let it in."

"Yes," George smiled. "You yourself had to be ready to receive it also. You see, it works both ways."

The subway train jolted once more.

"When will I be ready?"

"Sometimes we have to learn how to receive as much as we must learn how to give." George looked to the orb ahead. "What else can you remember?"

"All I can remember is my name, you know that already."

"Let go. Just be. Think of all we have seen on our journey together. Along all the stops we have made on this very train. Josh, I just want you to do just one thing."

"And what's that?"

"I want you to forget everything, and remember."

The same ease felt when meeting George for the first time came to Josh. He began to recount his journey.

"I remember the young couple," he began. "In the coffee shop where we watched their paths realign. I can remember the twin boys and their love for them. I remember the pain from the loss of their first child and how they were more concerned for the others sorrow than their own."

"Go on," George said. "Tell me more."

"I remember their first home together and the love that filled its small rooms. How they met in the train station and in the hospital hours later," he smiled. "Those wheels of fate wouldn't let them be, would they?"

"No, they wouldn't," George smiled too. "What else happened?"

"We watched them meet for the first time and fall in love. We saw them rediscover their Noa Koo again."

"What else, Josh?"

"There was the woman with the girl who smiled at you when she left the train. She looked so happy and content."

As the orb of light continued to hover outside the fluttering pages of the newspaper a few rows from him triggered fresh memories of his arrival onto the train.

"I can remember the young boy and, and I remember you," Josh continued. "I can remember sitting right here and you came up to me. You said my name."

"Go on, Josh."

"I remember sitting here alone in this subway car at an empty station. I didn't know where I was, or how I got there." He turned to George. "And I can remember that terrible car crash."

"What car crash, Josh?"

"The car crash. It seems dreamlike, but I know it's there. That it happened."

Josh's attention wavered on trying to remember more.

"Look deep within, Josh. What can you see?"

Josh leant forwards, his face in his hands. He sat up with a jolt.

"I can see the rain. It's so heavy. I can see the car lights ahead, everybody's rushing." He paused. "I can feel the impatience, the tension."

"What tension, Josh?"

"The tension in the car."

"And how does that feel?"

"It's unbearable." Josh looked to the subway car ceiling as lost memories flooded back to him.

"The road, it's wet, slippery. The rain's getting stronger. The car ahead. It's stopped," panic rose in Josh's voice. "I can't stop, I'm going too fast. It's too late, there's not enough time. Then…"

"Then what, Josh? Tell me what happened next."

"Then there was this bang as the cars hit each other. Then silence. It was so quiet." He swung round to George. "The car it's upside down, it's falling, we're falling."

"Who's falling?"

"All of us. Me, the boys and…" His eyes widened. "Sophia."

Josh stared ahead as the train rumbled and began to accelerate.

"Sophia," he said once more, oblivious to the sudden increase of speed.

"It has been a long journey to arrive here," George said at his side.

"I have to get back to them. Are they all right?"

George remained silent as Josh's eyes brimmed with tears.

"Are they ok?"

Waiting for an answer he sprung to his feet.

"Where are they?"

Continuing to look ahead George pointed behind Josh. In fear of who or what was behind him, Josh steadied himself and prepared to meet whatever waited at the end of the subway car. An empty carriage greeted him.

"What? There's nothing there," he said.

"Look closer, Josh."

His view settled on the discarded newspaper.

"This?" He swiped the paper up and turned back to George. "Is this what you want me to see?"

George gave no answer.

"Why aren't you helping me?"

"Oh, but Josh, I am."

"How? With this?" The newspaper trembled in his clenched fist.

Throwing the newspaper to the floor its loose pages scattered around his feet.

"Just tell me where they are. Where I am." Josh lowered his head. A single sheet of print lay across his shoes.

"Read what it says," George encouraged.

Picking up the sheet Josh slumped down next to George. Colour drained from him as he poured over its words. Reading the page once more he dropped it to the floor. Its headline stared back up at him, 'Family in near fatal accident' emblazoned across its top in bold black letters.

"That's us?" He asked as a breeze drifted through the subway car.

George nodded and watched the newssheet lift and glide along the aisle to the end of the subway car. It came to a rest below the rear window.

"What else did it say?" He asked.

"It says that they're ok. The boys, Sophia, but me." He paused and looked to the newspaper. "It says I'm…"

"It says what, Josh?"

"It says that I'm…well at least I'm not."

"Not what?"

"It says I'm critical. Does this mean I'm going back?"

"It is still up to you," George said. "If this is what you really want to do."

"Of course it's what I want," Josh snapped.

"How much, Josh? How much do you want to go back?"

The train accelerated once more. As its windows began to vibrate the noise around them grew in pitch.

"More than anything," Josh shouted out.

Feeling warmth across his cheeks he looked to the end of the carriage. The orb of light neared the carriage again. Josh leapt to his feet and ran down the aisle towards it.

"Let me in," he yelled at it.

Coming to a stop the orb floated outside. Josh looked over his shoulder to George.

"It is still up to you, Josh," he called to him.

"How?"

"You just have to want to receive it."

The noise in the train increased and its metal walls buckled and twisted as they hurtled faster through the tunnel.

"I want to receive it," Josh said into the light. "I want more."

Arms out stretched out on either side of him, he closed his eyes. "I want it all," he shouted up to the ceiling.

As the train continued to creak and groan around him the orb began to swell. It entered the subway car and rushed towards Josh.

The roar of the train ceased and Josh's sight glowed red behind closed eyelids.

"Josh," George whispered to him. "Open your eyes."

CHAPTER TWENTY-FIVE

Josh could taste the charges of energy filling the air. They buzzed and crackled around him as he lowered his arms and opened his eyes. Immersed in pure white light him George walked to him.

"Well done, Josh. You did it."

"Did what?"

"Josh," George swept a hand across the lit carriage. "You have arrived."

"Where? Where have I arrived?"

"Josh, you are exactly where you are supposed to be."

"Huh?"

George laughed to his response.

"You made it here, into the light. You let in and in turn it let you in also. The light only received you on seeing you were ready to receive it. For along this journey you have shown a willingness to see rather than merely just look. The light recognised this in you even if you did not yourself."

George stepped closer to Josh.

"Can you see what you have done? What you achieved? You have managed to disperse of all your prejudices, both willingly and voluntarily. You have shed old ways of seeing in order to be able to embrace new ways of thinking and doing."

Josh listened intently to his words.

"You have become more receptive to the world around you as it really is and have seen what is important in life. What truly matters."

"The ones we love," Josh looked into George's blue eyes. "The people in our lives. The way we give to each other and the way we must learn to receive too."

The subway car sizzled around him as he placed the pieces of his own puzzle together and told George of his discoveries.

"The lessons we learn from everyone we meet. Each with a message for us, good or bad. Everyone on his or her own path, their own journey through life. Each one with their own story, and how it is up to them whether to keep their story together with those they love and care for. That decision is all up to them."

Looking to the floor he realised the implications of his words to George and to himself.

"It's all up to me," he added.

Reaching out George put a hand on his shoulder. No words came from either. There was no need, Josh knew exactly where he had arrived.

He realised the destination he had so longed for had not been a physical location all along, but another place, a place hidden deep within him. Although George had been by his side throughout his journey his own thoughts and actions had brought him here. Here on this train, deep within the comfort of the orb's light.

"Yes," George said. "You discovered all this yourself. I was simply a guide to show you what you may have missed or forgotten. This is the way of things. Each and every one of us must discover or rediscover him or herselves at their own pace and can never be told."

"So we don't forget?" Josh said. "So I wouldn't forget."

"Yes, so you would not forget."

"So does this mean I'm going back?"

"Yes, you are going back to your own life. Remember how I said you had only been taken out of it? You are going back with all you have seen, all you have learnt. You have been given something so special, so precious. A second chance. But, remember that we are all learning, all the time. There is so much more for you to see and do yet. Your own unique path must continue onwards with you at its helm."

Josh looked to the subway car doors.

"Always remember that it is your story Josh, your choices in life, your decisions. Never forget this."

The light that had filled the subway car began to recede. It flowed and crackled its way over Josh and George. The train's speed decreased until a melodic hum as the orb hovered outside the subway car once more.

"Why has it left us?" Josh asked.

"It will return. You have received it once and so shall you again. And next time Josh it will be much easier for you. Come sit with me awhile."

Returning to the back of the subway car they took their seats once more. As the train slowed the orb edged closer, its rays trickling through the rear window and illuminating the loose newssheet below. Josh recalled its headline.

"The newspaper. It's been there all along."

"From the moment you first arrived on this train."

"So the answers were there all the time? Right in front of me?"

"All the time."

Josh couldn't understand why he had not noticed those answers straight away.

"But they wouldn't have meant much to me back then," he looked to the remainder of the newspaper's scattered pages. "Everything revealed to me stage by stage at my own pace. Only when I was ready."

"Only when you were ready. Some take longer than others to get where they are going. We are all finding our way through life as best we can. We all make mistakes along the way as much as we progress forwards. For even those on their true paths, the journey often turns out to be more interesting than the arrival."

"And what a journey it's been."

"Yes, it certainly has."

Settling back into his seat George sensed Josh's preoccupation.

"What is it, Josh?" He asked.

"The seats. Why are they all facing the same way?"

"I was wondering when you would ask me that again. It is how we go through our lives."

Josh stared ahead to the back of the seats before him.

"Josh, imagine yourself in a rowing boat out on the ocean."

"Is the sun shining?"

"Oh sometimes it is," George replied. "Sometimes," he smiled as he continued.

"As you row, you face the distant shore gradually flowing away from you. As does your past. And as you row steadily onwards your back is to the future. Uncharted waters hidden from view waiting to be explored and experienced."

Josh looked over the rows of orange and yellow plastic seats.

"The trick is, Josh, that no matter how rough or intimidating the ocean may become you must continue. You must keep rowing through the storms, the gales and lashing rains life sometimes throws at us until you reach calm and tranquil waters once more."

Josh's thoughts filled with Sophia and the boys.

"When do I go back?" He asked.

"Soon, Josh. Soon."

Excited by the prospect of being reunited with his family again he looked to the subway doors, imagining walking out through them with all he had learnt with George. Going back to his life, his second chance. That joy dimmed a little and he turned to George.

"I guess this is goodbye then?"

"Yes, Josh, it is. In a way."

"Are you coming with me?"

"I am, though not as such."

"What do you mean?"

"I have always been with you, Josh. From the moment you were born, when you re-entered this world and took your first tentative breaths," George smiled. "Throughout your childhood I was with you. I watched you emerge into adulthood and up until now, here in this present moment. And so shall I continue to do so until I stand by your side in the closing moments of your lifetime."

The train began to slow as Josh continued listening to George.

"Josh, you may not have seen me until we met here on this train, but I have always been with you. Have you not felt my presence at one time or another? Encouraging you onwards in your precious moments of joy and laughter?"

George glanced through the windows and returned to Josh.

"I was there when you took your first footsteps, as you discovered new tastes, smells and sounds as a child. As the years flashed by I watched you fall in love and have children of your own, and in turn you watched them discover and explore life for the first time as I did you."

Captivated by George's words Josh did not notice the train slow to a crawl.

"I have always been there Josh, through hard times as well. I sat next to you in those dark periods when you thought all was lost. I was there all along. Willing you onwards to keep on rowing until those stormy rain clouds above you lifted and you found yourself in calm still waters once more."

"Always?" Josh whispered.

"In your times of happiness and sorrow," George nodded. "When I see that things are running smoothly and you are heading where you are supposed to I leave you be, let you run free knowing all is fine with you. But I am always there, waiting in the wings so to say." George paused. "All you ever have to do is ask for me and I will be there with you."

Peace entered Josh in knowing he had never been alone.

"I have sometimes felt someone there," he said. "It was you wasn't it?"

George gestured to the windows beside them as their train eased into another empty station and came to a complete stop.

"Am I ready?" Josh asked.

"Yes, you are. You are ready to continue your adventure. Because Josh, that is what life is. An adventure to be grasped tight, embraced and enjoyed. Lived to the full."

George's eyes glistened as the orb's light reflected across them.

"You are going back equipped with all that you have learnt at my side. To face the rest of your future with the same courage and openness you have shown here along this journey of yours."

Warmth flushed across Josh's cheeks. He looked to the orb as it crept towards them. It wavered in the centre of the subway car once more. George smiled into the light then turned to Josh.

"The sometimes difficult challenges encountered in life should not be seen as setbacks or tragedies, for they are life, Josh. They are there to be experienced as much as the good times. These experiences are the individual threads which make up our life story. These threads weave, entwine and slowly evolve into the rich tapestry that reveals all we have done in our lives. It is up to us how colourful and intricate these patterns become." George looked over to the subway doors. "Yes I know," he said. "They are still closed."

"But why? I'm ready now."

"Patience," George smiled. "There is someone I would like you to meet first."

CHAPTER TWENTY-SIX

Josh stared across the subway car for its new passenger.

"Who's here?" He asked.

Raising a finger to his lips George looked to the orb hovering in the centre of the subway car.

"He is ready to meet you now," he said.

The orb began to crackle and a dark speck appeared at its base. The dot grew bigger until a small tattered baseball shoe pushed through its surface. On stepping down into the aisle one leg followed another until a young boy emerged from the light and stood in the middle of the subway car.

Recognising him as the child he had laughed with at the start of his journey, Josh looked to the boy's mop of brown hair as he stared around his new surroundings, his blue jeans and colourful striped T-shirt in vivid focus against the orb's pure white backdrop.

The light's crackle subdued and the young boy looked ahead to Josh and George. He began to giggle.

"Josh," George said. "Go and say hello."

Josh left his seat and squatted down on his heels to be at eye level with their new passenger. "Hello," he said. "And what's your name?"

"Josh," the boy answered.

Startled not only by his answer but by the realisation of who this small boy could be, Josh stared into the child's eyes.

"Josh," George called.

"Yes," both Josh's replied. The young Josh started to giggle once more.

"Is he?" The elder Josh said.

"Do you not recognise yourself?" George walked to them. "Yes, this is you. Or at least a part of you that you may have forgotten."

Studying the younger version of himself, the boy's tousled hair, blue jeans and sneakers all reminded him of times past. He focused on the green and yellow bands looping around his T-shirt.

"I remember I was nine years old. This T-shirt, I wore it nearly every day one summer."

"Yes, I remember too," George nodded.

"The summer by the lake. A long hot dry summer," Josh recalled childhood memories. "I played from dawn 'till dusk."

"He is the essence of those times. Of that glorious summer you spent with your grandparents. Happy carefree days when all that mattered was the present moment." George's eyes fell to the young Josh listening intently to the adult's every word.

"It is good to see you again," George smiled to him.

The young child returned his smile.

"By that lake," George looked back to the older Josh. "It was a time when you thought each day would never end. Not once did you worry about those closing hours of sunlight which crept up on you. And when those hours of darkness arrived and playtime had come to an end? You accepted it, Josh. You accepted it with all your heart, as had you that very same morning as the sun rose and a new day of adventures were unleashed before you."

Smiling to his younger self, Josh recalled the happy moments of a summer spent by the lake, the woods he had keenly explored and how he had swam in the lake's peaceful waters every morning. Josh recalled fishing with his grandfather in the afternoon, recalling how he had not cared as the dimming light of evening had covered them both. For tomorrow was simply another day to him back then.

The young Josh became restless and went to discover the rest of the subway car. Climbing onto a row of seats to reach a map above them he followed an intricate criss-cross of lines, a small finger held inches away from his nose.

"Josh, he is you through and through," George said. "You conjured up his appearance from memories of times long ago. A time when you sought adventure and explored the world around you with no reservations whatsoever."

He smiled back to the boy now seated and engrossed in a discarded coffee cup found on his exploration.

"When all was new to you, Josh, you embraced life with great curiosity, open and receiving all around you. This younger self is that element of peace within you. The inner child you had forgotten and gradually left behind over the years."

George beckoned the young Josh to join them.

"He is the part of you that giggled and laughed with no worries of what the future may bring, the part of you that enjoyed living in the present with no thoughts of the past or unknown future, instinctively knowing how to just be. He is the one going back with you."

The subway car doors hissed and slid open. Staring onto the empty platform Josh felt a tiny hand slip into his. Looking down he was greeted by an excited smile.

"It is time, Josh," George said as the elder Josh turned to him, his eyes filled with tears. "Do not be sorrowful. For farewells are seldom important, it is the quality of time spent together which truly counts."

The young Josh pulled on his elder self's hand.

"He is ready," George said. "And so my friend, are you."

The orb crackled once more. It pushed forward over the three of them, filling the remaining carriage with light. Spilling out from the subway car's windows and doors it spread across the platform and into the station's outer reaches until all around became bathed in rich, pure whiteness.

The young Josh eyed the doors. He rushed towards them pulling his elder self in his wake. Josh stumbled forwards and stopped. His feet hung over the lip of the trains exit and he looked to the young Josh smiling up to him from the platform, his hand still clenched in his.

"Go on, he is waiting for you. It is all waiting for you, Josh."

Comforted by George his thoughts filled with all that lay before him, Sophia, the boys, and the knowledge that would now accompany him back there. He left the subway car and stepped onto the glowing platform.

Staring around the brightly lit station he turned to face the subway car. George smiled to him from its open doors.

"Thank you," Josh said.

"No, Josh," George shook his head. "You did it all yourself. I was only here to guide you, to reveal what you may have missed along the way. A certain way to be. Your way, Josh."

The understanding Josh had tried to reach throughout their journey came. He saw how George's small nudges and pushes had gently guided him to explore parts of himself never imagined before. Valuable lessons, all taught under a veil of patience and unconditional love through George's tender words.

The orb's light increased and both Josh's looked up to George. Only his shoulders and face were visible to them now.

"Namaste, Josh," George said out to him.

"Namaste, George," Josh watched his friend step back into the subway car and fade out of view.

Continuing to stare ahead in hope of a final glimpse of George, the light around Josh intensified and he began to grow tired.

Feeling the small hand in his squeeze tightly on his fingers he looked down to its owner. The light had become so strong he could no longer see his younger self and with a sleepy glance back to where George had stood Josh's eyes began to close.

CHAPTER TWENTY-SEVEN

JOSH'S DESTINATION

Monotone beeps sneaked into Josh's consciousness. Muffled at first they grew clearer as he regained his senses. The soft pillow beneath his head pushed down as he inhaled and smells of fresh linen drifted about him.

Josh tried to open his eyes. Their lids remained closed and he began to sit up. Then pain struck. His whole body ached and he lay back down between the realms of dream and reality once more, any new attempts to move dismissed from him.

His palm warmed as tiny fingers squeeze round his. Consoled in their gentle grasp his mind escaped back to the comfort of the subway car. His pain subsided and he slipped further into the remembrance of his journey. Thoughts of the young couple, his younger self and George's kindness came.

The beeps beside him rose in tempo. They re-entered his awareness, dragging him back into painful reality.

Withstanding the pain as much as possible Josh coaxed himself to move again and shuffled sideways. His left arm jarred and he reached over to it with the other. With the sounds of footsteps rushing towards him he stroked over the numerous tubes tugging at his skin. His arm fell back to his side as hurried footsteps ran from him only to return seconds later accompanied by several others.

Cold touches poked and prodded him. Josh sensed panic in the air. He flinched to the sharp line drawn up the sole of his foot from heel to toe, searching deep within to unlock the barrier guarding his vision.

Delving deeper for the keys to his sight, his answer appeared in the cry of a child. It was soon joined by another's tiny wail. They echoed around him. Then somebody said his name.

"Josh," a woman's voice called. "Josh, can you hear me?"

The voice's familiar tone coupled by children's cries gave Josh the final push needed. His eyes opened and light flowed back into his world again.

"Josh, I'm here, we're all here."

He looked up to blurred bodies around his bed.

"Talk to him," one of the figures said. "He needs you."

The small hand in Josh's wriggled and a childlike giggle played in his ears. Grasping the hand it transformed into long delicate fingers which stretched out and curled around his. Josh gazed up at the features now leaning over him framed by unmistakable red hair.

"Josh, you're going to be ok."

Josh smiled back up to her.

"We're here now," she said. "It's all here, just waiting for you."

Cool strands of hair danced across Josh's neck as a tear fell onto his cheek.

"I missed you," Sophia whispered to him.

Josh smiled once more as her tender lips kissed him on the forehead.

"Namaste," he whispered up to them. "Namaste."

CHAPTER TWENTY-EIGHT

NEW BEGINNINGS

"Happy Birthday," chorused throughout the room.

Over tips of tiny flames Josh looked at the cake placed before him then to each of his family seated around a food-laden table.

One by one, the twins, their wives and his granddaughter all greeted him with a smile. His eyes met with Sophia's beside him.

Her hand slipped into his and squeezed tight, the reflection of the dining room's roaring log fire in her eyes, licks of fire dancing across deep dark brown pools still filled with life after all these years.

"Come on Grandpa, blow the candles out," their granddaughter called from across the table.

"Yes, come on, Grandpa," Sophia teased.

Josh looked to the blazing cake. He took a moment before looking to his family, confused by the request.

"I can't," he told them.

The room fell silent and Sophia shuffled anxiously in her seat.

"Why not, Josh?"

"This can't be my cake."

"Of course it's your cake, sweetheart. Who else's birthday is it?"

Looking to his family once more he was greeted by concerned faces from all present.

"But it can't be mine," he continued.

"Of course it's yours dad," one of the twins said. "Whose cake do you think it is? Why do you think we're all here, together?"

He glanced over to his mother, worried about his father's confused state.

"Well I don't think it's mine because…" Josh gave all a youthful grin betrayed only by fine wrinkles around green eyes. "Because there are more than twenty-one candles on it."

The table erupted into laughter, tinged with relief.

"Josh," Sophia suppressed her smiles.

"And anyway," Josh continued. "I can't blow them out until my grandson gets here."

"Oh, he will be here," his other son said.

"Yes, Josh, he's not going to miss his Grandpa's seventy-fourth birthday is he?" Sophia said. She turned to her daughter in-law.

"Is he finally going to introduce us to this new girlfriend of his?"

"Sarah? Oh yes, she's coming too."

"Sarah," Sophia's eyes sparkled in anticipation to their new guest's arrival.

"Well they'd better be quick," Josh nodded to half melted sticks of wax. He looked up as the front door opened, slammed shut and footsteps rushed towards them.

"Sorry we're late," their grandson burst into the room. "Happy birthday, Grandpa."

"Just in time," Sophia turned to Josh. "Now Grandpa, are you going to blow these candles out, or am I?"

Leaning forwards and with one breath Josh blew them all out. Cheers broke out around the table. Behind silver trails of smoke Josh heard his grandson call out over the applause.

"Grandma, Grandpa, this is..."

"Sarah," Sophia welcomed and patted the seat next to her. "Come sit next to me. Josh, make room for the young lady."

Shuffling sideways Josh peered through the last remnants of smoke. He froze as the haze lifted to unveil Sarah to him.

"Josh?" Sophia whispered, puzzled by his reaction.

Josh glanced back to her and continued to move aside. His gaze fell back to Sarah as she took her place beside Sophia. His wife gave him a frown and then turned to their grandson's girlfriend.

"What a beautiful hair you have," she said to Sarah. "I can remember when mine was as red as yours, many years ago," Sophia ran her fingers through shoulder length grey locks.

"Remember, Josh?"

Josh nodded, his view still on Sarah.

"Better watch this one. He likes his redheads," Sophia said, her squeeze on Josh's hand increasing as she spoke.

"And Sarah, what a lovely name."

"Thank you, it's my grandmother's." Sadness played across Sarah's delicate features and she bit into her bottom lip. "Well, was her name," she added.

"I'm sorry, sweetheart." Sophia said.

Nodding to thank her for her kindness, Sarah looked around the dining table. Josh watched her observe his family as they chatted and laughed amongst themselves. He leant over to her.

"Tell us about your grandmother, Sarah," he asked.

"Josh," Sophia was surprised by his forwardness.

"No, it's ok," Sarah reassured. "I like to talk about her, it kind of still keeps her alive, you know?"

Sophia and Josh settled back as Sarah told them of her grandmother.

"She passed away peacefully three months ago," she began. "My grandfather was there by her side. Holding her hand the way he had always done for as long as I can remember."

"And how is he coping?" Sophia asked.

"Oh, you know, he's ok. He misses her terribly of course, more than he likes to admit I reckon. They never spent a day apart for forty-five years." She paused. Her face lit up. "He always says how much he's looking forward to them finding each other again. Next time around he says, like they do every lifetime."

Tears welled in Sophia's eyes and she smiled to Josh.

"He says he wonders where they will be when they recognise each other again. And he often talks of the big lake where they first met."

"That sounds wonderful," Sophia said.

"Yeah, soul mates and all that," Sarah smiled.

"Noa Koo," Josh whispered.

Sarah stared over at him.

"Yeah, Noa Koo. That's what they used to call each other. How do you…"

Sarah stopped. She saw that the whole table had listened to her tale, enchanted by her every word. "So," she blushed. "How long have you guys been married for?"

"Forty-five years," Josh replied, still stunned by Sarah's recollections of her grandparents.

"Forty-two, Josh," Sophia corrected. "Remember?"

Josh had never told Sophia of George and their journey together on the subway train. Instead he had used the knowledge discovered then wisely throughout the years.

In those early days after Josh had awoken from the accident Sophia and he had talked honest and true of their feelings for each other. They both came to a unique decision. They decided to start their life together afresh, a new start for them both. From that moment onwards there was no talk of their past. Only the present mattered, accompanied by their dreams of a future together.

It had been hard for them at first, but gradually not talking of their life before the accident developed into a game, with each one pulling the other one up if they slipped into the past, their past. It soon turned into a competition, and as they played together it only strengthened the bonds between the two.

The years rolled by and new experiences formed new memories to fill the gaps of their past, until not talking of their time together before the accident simply became a way of life for them both.

"Forty-two years," Josh said to Sarah.

Rising to his feet he smiled down to Sophia. Giving her a kiss on her forehead he watched Sophia's cheeks flush crimson.

"And where are you going, young man?" She smiled up to him.

"Just going to get some air," he walked towards the porch door.

Turning to his family Josh looked to Sarah.

"Thank you for telling us of your grandmother," he said to her.

"You're welcome," Sarah smiled and watched Josh continue to the door.

Its handle in his grasp Josh paused again.

"Hey Grandma," he heard his grandson call. "Guess what? Sarah's dad's a twin too."

"Really? Tell us more."

Sophia's excited tones drifted from Josh as he walked out onto the porch. In late afternoon autumn sunlight he closed the door behind him.

Cool breezes whipped golden leaves high up into the air. Josh watched them escape and flutter from the semi-bare trees of the woods in the near distance. The winds picked up and his view followed a trail of orange and yellow dancing along the path of his and Sophia's lakeside home until coming to rest next to still waters.

Making his way to the porch's large wicker couch, the wooden floorboards beneath him creaked under his slow pace. Easing himself back amongst soft down cushions he looked out onto the lake, its glassy sheen glimmering in the onset of a day's fading light.

Josh couldn't believe how quick the last ten years had passed since he and Sophia had made this their home. The city of their youth seemed so far from the peaceful days they now spent together, here beside the lake in the closing chapters of their lives.

Muffled laughter flowed from the house and Josh's thoughts turned to Sarah. How could it be possible? So many years had passed, but his journey with George had remained with him every day since they had parted.

He had always been able to conjure up memories of those times in an instant. They were as clear and distinct to him now as if yesterday.

He had recognised Sarah's likeness from the first moment she appeared. Her presence to him was unmistakable. Could it have been the grandmother she had talked so fondly of? Could it really be? Josh battled within him.

He willed his memories to cloud over so he could believe what he always had. That it had been his and Sophia's story, no one else's. Yet, no matter how hard he tried those recollections remained vivid to him with untarnished sharpness.

Seeing how the young man he had watched grow throughout his formative years had in fact formed the man he had become, Josh's whole attitude to life had been moulded by what he had witnessed. He realised how his morals and actions all pivoted on him.

A sudden rustle of leaves from the porch steps diverted Josh from his internal questioning. Two tiny ears rose up from a bed leaves. Green eyes followed and looked down to the small black paws stretched out before them.

The cat mewed, stretched once again and then padded her way to Josh. Finding a home in his lap she cradled in his warmth and returned to her nap. Stroking the warm bundle Josh looked out onto the lake. A strong gust of wind broke his peace.

Branches creaked and groaned from the woods and the cat stirred and sat up. Her head darted to the trees. Leaping from Josh's lap she paced over to the porch's top step and stared into the woods.

"What can you see, girl?" Josh followed her stare.

She turned back to Josh, purred and then returned to look into the woods beyond. Between its trees something caught Josh's eye also.

In the distance a blurred shape drifted in and out of view.

The blur developed into a figure and walked towards the house.

Josh rose to his feet ready to greet the solitary person. Another tourist lost in the woods he guessed and smiled to the man emerging from the tree line. Josh's welcome was replied by a brief wave.

Peering closer Josh's smile turned into astonishment as the cat purred at his feet then ran over to the approaching man.

"This sure is a day for surprises," Josh said.

The cat purred again as the unexpected arrival crouched down and stroked beneath her chin.

"Yes, Josh," George said. "It certainly is."

CHAPTER TWENTY-NINE

OLD FRIENDS

Standing atop the porch steps Josh stared into George's blue eyes. So many years had passed since they had said goodbye, yet his old friend retained his ageless quality, his appearance no different now than what Josh remembered from decades ago. George looked over Josh's shoulder.

"Shall we?" He nodded to the wicker couch. Climbing the steps he placed a helping hand beneath Josh's arm on their walk together.

"Thank you," Josh said to him.

The couch creaked as they both eased back and looked to the lake. They sat in comfortable silence. The way they had done a lifetime ago. George winked to the cat watching them from the foot of the steps. Tilting her head to one side, she vaulted onto the porch and jumped into George's lap. She snuggled down and closed her eyes.

"Another birthday, Josh," George listened to muffled laughter coming from the dining room. "And a new visitor too, I see."

"You mean, Sarah?"

George nodded.

"She seems so," Josh searched for the right word.

"Familiar?"

"Very familiar. Was her grandmother... Was she the young woman?"

George smiled to him again.

"Does it really matter, Josh? Would it have made any difference to your life if the young woman had been Sarah's grandmother, or Sophia?"

"I don't know? I mean, I've just always believed that..."

"Believed?"

"Yes, believed that the young couple. That they were us, Sophia and me."

"Believed," George repeated. "Josh that is what you had to do, all you have ever had to do. Just believed."

Josh listened to George as attentively as he had when a younger man.

"For when we first met on that subway train, Josh, your ability to believe was a part of you that had been lost. Locked away and hidden deep within yourself. Tell me, how long has it been now?"

"Forty two years."

"Forty two years," George echoed as he watched a group of leaves swirl inches above the ground. "To me it has been the blink of an eye, but moments since we last talked together." George looked to the house and then to Josh. "Look how far you have come, how well you have done. You began to believe again. You gave your second chance all you had, rekindling the belief inside you that anything was possible."

Laughter flowed once more from the house and its party within. George glanced back to the door.

"You believed in yourself, and in time began to believe in others too. In turn your dreams of the future flooded back to you in forms of reality."

Listening to his family's happy sounds in the background, Josh's thoughts filled with memories of the last four decades.

"Belief that anything is possible is always within us, within us all," George said. "Noa Koo, soul mates, happiness and all your heart desires. All these things can happen and invariably do as long as the doors to our dreams are kept open, believing we can achieve anything, no matter how unobtainable it may seem."

"And we start with ourselves," Josh said. "To have belief unlocks everything and opens the doors of possibilities to you."

George looked out to the lake's shimmering surface.

"Over the years I have watched you. I saw that however hard the challenges you came across were your belief in yourself and trust in those around you conquered all. Your dreams and aspirations were never far from reach were they? They were always within your grasp because you believed that anything is possible."

"And I felt you there with me in those times," Josh's eyes

glistened. "I really did."

"You see now, do you not? That we learn from the actions of others all around us. With the foundation of our own self-belief, each and everything we witness helps us grow into the singular, special souls we are. It is up to us how wisely we utilize these observations of others. It is up to us what knowledge and insights into life we choose to blend together with our own unique thoughts, ways and actions."

"So all I saw back then, along all those stops with you was?"

"Entirely for your own interpretation, Josh."

"But…"

George placed a hand on Josh's shoulder. Sensing peace flowing through him, he recognised the sensation not only from his younger years when last at George side, but also from certain challenging moments throughout his life since. Josh smiled back to George in understanding.

Sophia's laughter ran from the house. Looking to the porch door Josh listened to the carefree giggles of his Noa Koo.

His smile faded as he turned back to George.

"What is it, Josh?"

Taking a breath Josh stared at his old friend.

"You told me many years ago that you were there when I entered this world, and how you have always been by my side."

Josh glanced back to his family's laughter and then out onto the lake. In the day's closing light he watched swallows swoop down and skim across its surface. Above them a darkening sky revealed three flickering stars signalling the beginnings of a new night. As other stars emerged to accompany them he looked back to George.

"Is it time?" He asked.

George took Josh's hand in his.

"You have seen and experienced so much," he said. "During your time here you have learnt so many lessons."

Josh looked down to his hand safe and secure in George's.

"But one lifetime is so very short," George continued. "There is only so much we can discover to prepare us for the next. Do not be sad for you have come so far, and," George smiled, "there is still further for you to go."

"You mean?"

"Yes, Josh, there is still a little bit more for you to see yet."

Sophia's voice came from the house.

"Grandpa," she called.

"Come on Grandpa, they are all waiting for you," George laughed. Placing the cat down at his feet he lifted himself from the couch.

Josh accepted George's helping hand and stood too.

"Josh?" Sophia called again.

"Better hurry," George nodded to her voice and the cat's eager scratches at the base of the porch door.

"Goodbye, Josh," he smiled. "Until next time," he added before descending the porch's wooden steps and towards the trees from where he had appeared.

Beneath the moonlight of a cloudless night George waved back to Josh once before disappearing into the shadows.

An impatient purr sounded out behind Josh.

Looking down to her he walked to the door. Turning its handle he pushed it ajar and the cat darted inside as rich warmth greeted Josh from the party within.

He paused and looked back to the woods where he had last seen George.

"Namaste," he whispered out to them, and then with a smile returned to join his family.

The End.

ALSO BY THE AUTHOR

BY WAY OF THE SEA

One Monk's Journey of Discovery

A novel
Julian Bound

Struggling with his beliefs a Tibetan Buddhist monk begins a journey to see the sea he has always dreamt of. Travelling on foot through Tibet, Nepal and India to reach his goal, those he encounters along the way start to restore a faith lost to him.

After visiting Namsto Lake as a young novice, Tenzin has longed to stand before seas never witnessed in a landlocked Tibet. Coming of age he leaves Lhasa's Gyuto Monastery and travels southwards on his quest. Travelling through his homelands he walks beside holy lakes and over high attitude mountain passes until reaching Nepal's border.

Continuing south to Kathmandu and to Pokhara's sacred lake he arrives to the town of Lumbini on Nepal's border with India. There within the gardens of Buddha's birthplace Tenzin's fading beliefs begin to be rekindled.

Crossing into India he journeys south once more and soon meets with a path he is destined to take.

Encountering many on his travels each hold a valuable lesson for Tenzin as together they explore the concepts of attachment, impermanence, kindness and compassion and karma and reincarnation. With each insight gained he continues onwards, his pursuit to see the sea accompanied by a want to understand the faith in which he has been raised.

LIFE'S HEART ETERNAL

A novel
Julian Bound

'My name is Franc Barbour. I was born on the 20th July 1845 in the town of Saumur, deep in the heart of the Loire Valley, France. The truth of the matter is I simply never died.'

These are the opening words a young nurse reads in an old leather bound journal given to her by a stranger. She soon uncovers the story of one man's journey through the centuries.

Following Franc's path from 1845 until present day, 'Life's Heart Eternal' is a tale of how our actions in each lifetime often hold consequences in the next.

With Franc's travels across the world in his endless years, the reader anticipates his next encounter with those reincarnated from his past and of what lessons each shall meet with.

For who has never wondered what it would be like to live forever?'

THE GEISHA AND THE MONK

Two souls born thousands of miles apart
each shall follow a similar path

A novel
Julian Bound

KYOTO, JAPAN 1876: a girl is born into a lineage of famous geishas. Following her upbringing and training within a Tokyo geisha house her true identity is at last revealed.

GYANTSE, TIBET 1876: a boy is born into a small farming community. Recognised to be the reincarnation of a revered Lama he is taken to Shigatse's Tashi Lhunpo Monastery, it is there his unique destiny is unveiled.

SAN FRANCISCO, USA 1900
At the dawning of a new century fate brings them together, a lifetime away from all they have ever known.

With their stories running in parallel, *'The Geisha and The Monk'* tells of the training of a Tokyo geisha and a Tibetan Buddhist monk. Although coming from different backgrounds both share a matching destiny, one discovered when meeting on the shores of San Francisco's harbour front.

'Eventually, two souls destined to meet shall do so, their connection instantly
recognised within the eyes of the other.'

THE SOUL WITHIN

*Because everyone longs for
their soul to be touched*

A novel
Julian Bound

Falling ill in his home town of Puri on India's eastern coastline, a boy is visited by his spirit guide. Taking him on a journey around a tranquil lake, together they observe those living along its banks.

As his guide explains the life lessons they encounter through her subtle teachings, the boy's emerging awareness to matters of the soul leads him to discover the reasons behind their meeting as his story unfolds.

A heart-warming tale of awareness, 'The Soul Within' offers its readers an insight into another's awakening, guided by the love and kindness held within us all.

*In releasing our thoughts towards a lifetime imagined,
only then may we have the life our soul awaits.*

NON-FICTION

THE SEVEN DEADLY SINS AND THE SEVEN HEAVENLY VIRTUES

As viewed in religion, ancient mythology and art and literature

Julian Bound

The Seven Deadly Sins and the antidotes of the Seven Heavenly Virtues have been depicted throughout history in forms of both Greek and Roman mythology and in the world of art and literature.

Perceived as being associated within the doctrine of the Christian faith, the eastern religions of Buddhism, Hinduism and Sikhism all share a parallel view of the seven sins and virtues, yet are expressed in the theology of different precepts.

'The Seven Deadly Sins and The Seven Heavenly Virtues' examines the similarities of each sin and virtue within religions of the world, and of the portrayal in mythology and art and literature.

'The Seven Deadly Sins and The Seven Heavenly Virtues' also invites the reader to identify which sin they are prone to and of what virtue best displays their greatest qualities; the result of which is an exploration of the self within the aspects of the seven sins and seven virtues, and so acting as a guide for each soul's unique individual path.

Printed in Great Britain
by Amazon